VICKSBURG

A Skirts to Swords Adventure

PAULA LENOR WEBB

A Skirts to Swords Adventure

ISBN:
Paperback 979-8-9905622-8-8
eBook 979-8-9905622-9-5

Azalea City Publishing, LLC
Mobile, AL 36693
www.azaleacitypublishing.com
Cover design: Artillery Design Company Ltd
https://www.artillerydesign.co.uk/

WWW.PLWEBB.COM

OTHER WORKS BY PAULA

Mobile Under Siege: Surviving the Union Blockade

Such A Woman: The Life of Madam Octavia Walton LeVert

Mississippi Mojo… and Murder: A Tale of the Blues

Devilry in the Delta: A Mississippi Mojo Thriller

Melody of Malice: A Mississippi Mojo Thriller

ACKNOWLEDGEMENTS

I would like to thank Mary S. Palmer, Shannon Brown, and David Preston for helping me keep the writing dream alive.

Chapter One

Rebecca perched on the silk-covered window seat; her gaze fixed on the bustling street below. The midday sun cast a warm glow as she looked for Mr. Wales W. Wood, Esq. from the window of her family's New York brownstone. Every nerve in her body tingled with anticipation.

He must pass by here soon. She leaned forward for a better view. A tinge of irritation crossed her mind as the housekeeper appeared, dusting the windowsill.

From her vantage point, Rebecca saw the comings and goings of the city's elite. Her father, Joseph Cashin II, had ensured their home was the grandest on the street, a testament to his success in the mercantile business. Today, she was on a mission—a mission to intercept Wales before he reached the home of Miss Alice Strong, the latest object of his affections.

I simply do not understand what he sees in her. She is so boring. She brushed away a bit of flour dust from her dress.

As she tapped her fingernails on the marble sill, her thoughts drifted to her father's words of wisdom. "Own where you lay your head and have the upper hand," his voice a constant presence in her mind. She interpreted his words to imply, "Find a man who can support a household, and you can control."

Rebecca's older sister had heeded his remarks and married Mr. R. H. Douglas of the Douglas family industries. Emily often flashed her diamond ring to remind Rebecca of the money and prestige that came with her new husband. It was irritating to hear her tales of meeting the Roosevelts or the Rockefellers. There was only one way to change the situation for Rebecca, and that was to marry someone with greater prominence.

The sound of the family housekeeper interrupted her as she dusted, bringing her back to the present. "Such a nice day, Miss Rebecca," Jenny remarked, her voice breaking Rebecca's concentration. She paid her little mind, her focus on the task at hand.

With a dismissive wave, Rebecca commented, "Can you do something else? You are quite distracting." Jenny mumbled apologies as she left the room. She contemplated her plan to intercept Wales before reaching Alice's doorstep and Rebecca knew the timing was crucial. She could not let this opportunity slip through her fingers.

Mr. Planters momentarily distracted her by yelling, "Fresh roasted peanuts! Get your peanuts here!" from his street cart two doors down. She could smell the rich aroma as it wafted towards her window. She pictured the delicious cookies made from roasted peanuts, mixing the batter, and then slipping them into the new oven her father bought for the kitchen. She could almost taste the fresh cookies as they melted into her mouth and the sweet taste…delectable!

Her mother, wanting Rebecca to be more lady-like, fussed when she was in the kitchen covered in flour or buying new spices from the street vendors. Rebecca knew it was the maid's responsibility to cook, but no one knew how to use the new stove like she did. She had to do something when Jenny burned the bread or overcooked the stew. Rebecca visited the New York Society Library and read everything she could on the topic.

This is no time to be hungry, she reflected, fingering the pages of the cookbook in her lap. She glanced again down the street one way and then the other, fearful she missed her moment. The grand facade of her home afforded her a perch for her favorite pastimes: observing people and gathering gossip.

As street vendors' carts danced amidst the pedestrian flow, she absorbed every tidbit of action. The Wells Fargo messengers, splendid in their crisp attire and gleaming badges, caught her attention as they delivered envelopes, whether of social invitations, private or professional correspondence.

With rumors of war between the states resurfacing, she wondered about the allegiances of her neighbors. Who aligned with the Federals, and who had thrown their lot in with the rebellious South, risking familial disgrace?

While intriguing tales and scandal found their way to her ears, on this day, she fixated on the dashing Wales W. Wood. Upon learning of his impending visit to Miss Alice Strong, she focused on her family residence three doors down and across the street. Wales must not tread that path today.

Or any day, if I can do something about it, Rebecca decided. She reached into the pocket of her dress and pulled out a white handkerchief. She fingered the initials, W.W.W., embroidered in one corner.

Mrs. Wales W. Wood or Mrs. Rebecca C. Wood? Undecided how she wanted her married name, it was an issue she could resolve later. Rebecca's cheeks burned at the memory of Wales at Madame LeVert's New York Salon, where they first met.

When she first saw Wales, he embodied the man Mrs. Gwin's Ladies School groomed her to attract and marry. Skilled in the art of hosting functions and orchestrating state dinners, Rebecca could work a room unlike any other. The same training school helped her sister capture her prize, but her new husband was not the type for Rebecca. *He is decent to Emily, but he will not do for me.*

Underlying Rebecca's accomplishments was her ability to observe those around her. She knew Wales had a promising future, but he was also indecisive and impulsive. However, these traits she could use to her advantage when they married.

Of course, I will have to convince him to marry me. I cannot understand why he has any interest in Alice when I know he cares for me, she pondered, smoothing the handkerchief in her lap.

Rebecca recalled the day they met at Madame LeVert's, where she engaged in boring conversations with courting gentlemen between dances, all while they nibbled on her renowned sugar cookies.

It was during one such tête-à-tête she saw Wales Wood, the latest addition to Bidwell & Strong. He was another eligible bachelor in the societal market. In the first moments of the meeting, their dialogue dived into topics such as life's intricacies, philosophical musings, and the challenges they faced. Rebecca found the moment almost magical.

As Wales savored Rebecca's homemade delicacies, the depth of their conversation captivated her, challenging her impression of him. She felt the spark of attraction; she noticed the glint of interest in his bright blue eyes.

"Miss Cashin, I believe you have a crumb on your cheek," he said and handed her a white handkerchief.

Her cheeks went red in a blush as she wiped off the offending bit of cookie. She tried to give the handkerchief back, but he raised his hand in refusal. She placed it in her dress pocket, and where it remained with her since.

There was a flicker of appeal. She knew there was, so why was he compelled to visit Alice?

*　　*　　*

Upon recounting her meeting with Wales to her father, his eyes lit, making a note of the name for inquiry. He advised, while munching on one of her small cakes, "We must discover who he truly is behind closed doors." Using his mercantile business as a pretext, Joseph Cashin orchestrated occasions for Wales to visit their home for paperwork deliveries.

Without fail, Rebecca greeted him at the door over the next few weeks, bearing snacks to welcome him. He stayed to talk with her sometimes, but then, other times, he politely refused her invitation, leaving to visit Alice's home.

This will not do! She fumed as she watched their housekeeper let him in.

To delve deeper into Wales's character, Rebecca's father arranged for a maid, Nancy—sister to their live-in housekeeper, Jenny—to tend to Wales Wood's bachelor pad at Barlow House, the closest residence for unmarried lawyers. Within days, Nancy provided a trove of observations. They learned Wales devoted long hours to his work at the firm and exhibited a penchant for untidiness.

"Yes ma'am," Nancy reported to Rebecca, "He leaves his clothes in a heap on the floor when he comes home and eats out mostly. I tried to tidy up, but he could do better. He lives quite simply. I do not see any letters from a family anywhere. He saves his money and if he entertains the ladies…you know what I mean…then it is not at his place."

Rebecca listened closely. While Wales was not a rake like his friend Darcy, he was still visiting both Alice and herself. It was as if he were trying to choose between them, though he had not directly told her this—and, according to the gossip, he had said nothing similar to Alice. *True to form, he is not the best at deciding. Not a problem. I can remedy this for him later.*

She considered these behaviors as trivial matters, but it was through Nancy's recent revelation that caused her to act urgently. Wales's next visit to Alice Strong was to propose marriage. Discreetly pocketed her reward, Nancy assured Rebecca of Wales's decision, citing his conversation with Darcy as evidence just that morning.

*   *   *

While Wales's affections might lean towards Alice, Rebecca knew she could win him away if she had enough time. She strategized on how best to interfere. If Wales approached from Bidwell & Strong, he would round the corner from the east, passing her home first. This provided an opportunity for Rebecca to intercept him before he reached Alice's residence.

If he walked west from his apartment, he would head straight to Alice's, bypassing Rebecca's home. The direction of his approach would dictate her next move. If he came from the law firm, she could intercept him before he reached Alice's doorstep. But if he left his apartment, her plan remained uncertain. With time slipping away, Rebecca readied herself to act. She was determined to steer events in her favor.

As a blond-headed street vendor selling sweetmeats blocked her view; Rebecca's heart skipped a beat, but relief washed over her as the vendor passed, leaving her line of sight unobstructed. Fixated on the white door of the brownstone three buildings down where Alice Strong lived, an undercurrent of frustration simmered within Rebecca.

If only that meddling Alice would stay out of my way, Rebecca lamented.

One of her father's sayings echoed in her mind: "If you want something in this world, take it. No one is going to give it to you." She knew all too well how her family saw her—unlike the demure Alice or the quiet determination of her sister, Rebecca possessed a boldness that mirrored her father's, a trait often criticized by her more conventional relatives. Her mother's admonitions against her insatiable ambitions—spending less time in the kitchen, more time at formal gatherings where prospects awaited—had long lost their sting. Rebecca had resolved to pursue her desires, undeterred by anyone's expectations.

Shifting on the window seat, Rebecca's gaze remained fixed on the street below as she awaited Wales's approach. In her mind, there was no room for second thoughts—she was determined to seize what she wanted. Consequences be damned.

* * *

With a magnetic presence that drew attention wherever he went, Wales Wood was captivating. His pale blue eyes, the color of the sky itself, paired with golden hair that seemed to glow with a halo effect, made him impossible to overlook. Towering at over six feet, he commanded any room with a blend of confidence and impeccable style, his every step leaving an impression few could forget.

Wales, admired by both unmarried and married alike, Rebecca did not mind others taking notice of him, yet she harbored a fierce resolve that no viable rival would come between her and his affection. Of all her competitors, Alice was the strongest contender for his attention—and it didn't hurt that Wales also worked for Alice's father, too.

Rebecca wrestled with her own jealousy, a feeling that did not escape those around her. Her father, always quick with advice, urged her to seize every advantage. "Don't let her win, my girl," he counseled. "That young man is a prize, and we want the best for our family. Use every tool you have, even a touch of allure. Talk to your sister—she always knew just how to manage things like this."

Her father's words echoed in her mind as Rebecca stood poised at the window, eyes fixed on the street below, eagerly awaiting any sign of Wales's approach. She did not need her sister's advice— Rebecca knew exactly what to do and how to set her plan in motion.

When he walked down her street, on his way to Alice's house, she, by coincidence, would leave out her front door to send a package to a friend. She knew he trusted his friend, Mr. Darcy, and news of his entanglement with Miss Alice would distract him. No, it was not true, but it gave Rebecca time to distract him and help him reconsider his plans.

As she spotted his tall, distinguished figure rounding the corner, emanating from the direction of the law office, Rebecca's heart quickened in anticipation. Clad in a flawlessly tailored suit, his blond locks catching the sunlight, Wales embodied an allure that stirred something deep within Rebecca's own heart.

Eager to make an impression on Wales and divert his attention from Alice, Rebecca sprang into action. Pausing at the foyer mirror, she carefully adjusted every detail, ensuring her appearance exuded effortless charm. After a quick pinch to her cheeks and a finishing touch to her auburn locks, perfectly arranged, she stepped out with the package in hand, poised and ready to intercept Wales at just the right moment.

As he drew near, Rebecca felt a surge of urgency. She descended the steps with deliberate grace, positioning herself so he could not miss her. "Why, hello, Wales!" she called, her voice lilting with just the right amount of sweetness. "You look positively dashing today!" But Wales seemed oblivious, his gaze distant and unfocused, a subtle frown shadowing his features. She bristled—he was thinking of Alice. A pang of frustration ran through her.

Refusing to let him pass without noticing her, Rebecca stepped boldly into his path, her heart pounding as she forced him to stop. "Mr. Wood!" she called again, louder this time, with a hint of playful allure that could melt stone. "What a delightful surprise to see you here today." The seconds ticked by as she held her breath, hoping for a spark of recognition in his eyes, determined that this encounter would leave him as captivated by her as she was by him.

Wales stopped abruptly, nearly colliding with Rebecca. She saw his eyes widening in surprise. A flurry of apologies tumbled from his lips as his hands instinctively reached out to steady her. "Oh, Miss Cashin! I am terribly sorry!" he exclaimed, his charm shining through. His gaze softened, and a warm smile curved his mouth. "But truly, it's always a delight to encounter such beauty on this street."

Rebecca felt her heart skip, the intensity of his gaze setting her pulse racing. For a fleeting moment, she felt certain her presence had worked its magic, drawing his attention away from Alice, even if briefly.

Rebecca jokingly met his gaze, "You flatter me too much, sir. Your words may just cause me to swoon." Wales's laughter deepened her embarrassment, but she reveled in their playful exchange.

Wales, ever the gentleman, teased back, "Then I shall have to be prepared to catch you, lest I bear the guilt of causing your collapse with my compliments." Rebecca played along, mimicking a fainting spell as he kept his hands on her shoulders, indulging in their shared moment of amusement.

With a mischievous glint in her eye, Rebecca urged him to spare her further flattery. "Come now, tell me of your day and spare me more honeyed words lest I dissolve completely." As they spoke, Rebecca could not shake the feeling that perhaps her plan to divert Wales's attention from Alice was already beginning to bear fruit.

As Wales's arms dropped to his sides, his demeanor shifted to one of resignation as he recounted to her his day. "Very well," he conceded. "I shall be as dull as dishwater. Today I reviewed contracts, filed paperwork, and drafted dry legal briefs. Does that help steady you, my dear?"

Rebecca sensed his gaze drifting toward Alice's brownstone behind her, but she was determined to keep his attention. With a playful giggle, she gently rested her hand on his arm, feigning enthusiasm for his workaday topics. "Immensely! I am a rock under your mundane talk," she exclaimed. "Please, go on about clause amendments and witness statements. I drink it all in! My father talks of the same, and I could listen to him for hours."

Wales looked at her with eyes wide and was taken aback by her eagerness. "I'm afraid I'm too parched for legal jargon." He attempted to extricate himself politely. "Might I entice you to talk more about this later? I am going to see Miss Alice. Please excuse me."

Rebecca's heart sank as she realized he was intent on continuing to Alice's residence. She knew she had to act to prevent him from slipping away.

Feeling the urgency of the moment, Rebecca seized Wales's arm, halting his departure. "Wait, Mr. Wood!" she exclaimed, her voice tinged with seriousness. "Before you go, I feel I must warn you."

Her pull on his arm slowed him down and Wales obliged. "Of course, Miss Cashin. Regarding?" Rebecca noted his slight impatience, interpreting it as a sign that her ploy might work.

Glancing around to ensure they were alone, Rebecca leaned in close, her hand grasping his collar as she pulled him down to her level, her lips tantalizingly close to his ear. She could feel her heart racing as she inhaled his intoxicating scent.

Summoning her resolve, Rebecca whispered conspiratorially, "I overheard the most delicious piece of gossip." She knew Wales did not follow hearsay, but on this occasion, she hoped to use it to prolong their interaction.

"Oh?" Wales raised an eyebrow. "Do tell." Despite his reservations, Rebecca could sense a flicker of interest in his eyes, giving her hope her gambit might yet succeed.

Rebecca's heart pounded with anticipation as she spun her tale, her fingers smoothing a nonexistent wrinkle on Wales's collar. "Well," she began, her voice hushed with dramatic flair, "I heard from a reliable source that Mr. Darcy has been courting Miss Alice in secret!" She gasped, feigning shock. "Can you imagine, with their families being such rivals? It is scandalous."

Wales's eyes widened in disbelief, leaning in to catch every word. "No! Darcy and Alice? I never would have imagined." She managed to pique his curiosity. "Who told you this bit of gossip? I must know if it is true."

Rebecca maintained her facade of secrecy, playfully locking her lips as if to protect their identity. "I'm afraid my sources are confidential," she teased, a coy smile playing on her lips. "But I assure you, I have it on very good authority."

She observed with satisfaction as curiosity clouded Wales's features, his desire for confirmation clear. "I'm sure with your connections, you might know who told me," She continued brightly, her tone inviting.

Tilting her head inquisitively, Rebecca watched as Wales grappled with the revelation, sensing his uncertainty. "What do you say?" she proposed, her voice sweet with persuasion. "Join me for tea and cookies at the house, and we can compare notes. I am sure together we can uncover the truth." Anxiously, she awaited his response, hopeful that her invitation would serve as the final lure to keep him by her side.

As suspicion crept into Wales's expression, Rebecca felt a surge of panic rising within her. She had pushed it too far, and now she had to scramble. "That's quite an accusation, Miss Cashin," he remarked, his tone tinged with skepticism. "While I appreciate your...concern... I find it hard to believe Mr. Darcy would act in such an ungentlemanly fashion towards Miss Strong. I talked to him this morning, in fact, and he said nothing."

Rebecca blinked, realizing she needed to fabricate further to keep Wales engaged. "I assure you," she replied hastily, "my sources saw Darcy arrive at Alice's home just yesterday with a massive bouquet of roses! He is clearly intending to steal her away from under your nose."

Wales regarded her with a discerning gaze, his suspicion clear. "Indeed? How do you know I am interested in her?" he queried, his voice dropping to a whisper. "Then who are these mysterious sources of yours? Is it Alice? Is she spreading rumors we are engaged?"

Surprised, Rebecca stumbled over her words, her mind racing for a plausible response. "Well, I... I could not possibly..." she stammered, her facade crumbling under Wales's scrutiny.

"Come now, Miss Cashin," Wales interjected, his tone firm. "We discussed morals and foundational truths just the other day. If you want me to believe such scandalous gossip, you must reveal your sources." His words hung heavy in the air, leaving Rebecca grappling with the consequences of her deceit. She knew she had to think fast to salvage the situation and maintain her grasp on Wales's attention.

As Rebecca's lie fell flat, her desperation mounted. "Why... it was not Alice... it was Alice's own maid who told me!" she insisted, fabricating another falsehood to salvage the situation. "She informed me all about Darcy's secret courting."

Wales's response was icy, his demeanor imposing as he stepped closer, invading her personal space. "Did she now?" he retorted; his voice laced with skepticism. "Because I know Alice is lacking a maid. The last one became sick, and they are looking for a new one. While an imaginary person cannot say such things, I expect you and maybe Miss Alice, in fact, to be capable. Exercising your husband-hunting skills on yet another bachelor. Luring yet another sorry soul into a cage of decorum and wealth."

Rebecca recoiled, her heart sinking as she realized the depth of Wales's insight. Despite her initial attraction to his sharp intellect, she now found herself overwhelmed by his scrutiny. His flushed face betrayed restrained anger, hinting at emotions she could not decipher.

Wales sighed, shaking his head. "Miss Cashin, I appreciate your... enthusiasm. But did you think I would not recognize such a ploy? The two of you have joined forces to play me for a fool?"

Caught in the grip of Wales's rebuke, Rebecca's facade crumbled, leaving her speechless under his scrutiny.

"What do you mean?" She blinked, faking innocence.

"I think you know what I mean," Wales snapped, his tone unforgiving. "You enjoy making up malicious gossip, playing me into a game you are concocting. But I do not take kindly to deception."

Rebecca could only hang her head, imitating shame, knowing that any attempt to salvage the situation would be futile.

"Now, if you'll excuse me, I will go," Wales declared, his voice cold and final. "And in the future, I suggest you find other ways of spending your time."

With that, he turned sharply and strode away, leaving Rebecca standing alone on the sidewalk. As she watched him disappear down the street, she realized she pushed Wales further away.

Crestfallen, but not defeated, Rebecca resolved to find another way to win Wales's heart. He was not married yet, and this was a small setback. With a heavy sigh, she retreated into her home when he left her sight. She closed the door behind her and steeled herself for the challenges that lay ahead.

Chapter Two

Wales turned the corner, slipping away from the stifling brownstones and their wealthy occupants. The crowded street felt like a cage. He flagged down a cab to Bidwell & Strong on Wall Street, his mind churning over the chaos Rebecca had stirred up, each thought biting deeper as the cab rolled on. He decided he was done with all New York society women; both Rebecca and Alice.

Rebecca's behavior caught Wales off guard. Their first meeting at the salon intrigued him; she wasn't like the other women who flitted through society, or so he assumed. Wales, never one for dancing, preferred conversation, yet he hadn't expected to meet someone as captivating. She drew him in with her sharp wit and a refreshing lack of pretense.

Then there was her skill in the kitchen—another revelation. Most ladies in New York society wouldn't dare dirty their hands with this kind of work. But Rebecca moved through the kitchen with confidence, her movements practiced, her skill unmistakable. Her dishes weren't just food; they were small works of art, rich with flavors that could make even the finest chef envious.

Moved by his growing admiration, he presented Rebecca with a token—a handkerchief. For Wales, this gesture was meaningful. He rarely parted with his handkerchiefs, viewing them as personal items. However, in this instance, he felt compelled to share something special with Rebecca, hoping she would understand the depth of his sentiment.

The next day, he regretted it. For all her allure, Rebecca wasn't the woman a man of his station. When Wales mentioned her to his friend William Darcy, he received a swift warning: "Avoid that one, my man! She's wild—got a mind of her own. A woman who thinks for herself is nothing but trouble!" As Darcy's words echoed in his mind, Wales found himself drawn to her even more.

Yet, if Wales was to advance at Bidwell & Strong, he needed a well-connected wife. George Templeton Strong, one of the firm's managing partners, had implied this over cigars and brandy in his office one day, the room heavy with the scent of mahogany and ambition. Strong leaned in, his piercing gaze fixed on Wales, and said, "A man in your position, Wales, needs a solid foundation.

Connections, family, a wife who complements your drive. Someone like my daughter, Alice."

Within a week, Wales had lunch with Alice Strong at Delmonico's, the favored haunt of New York's elite. She was well-bred, poised, and polite—a model of society's expectations. As they dined, Alice spoke of her European travels, her charity work, and the latest social events, all with the grace expected of her station. The match would be a convenient one. Wales hardly minded an arranged marriage if it would lead to a partnership at the firm and secure his future.

But meeting Rebecca changed things. Alice's polished charm seemed pale against Rebecca's raw authenticity and the warmth she brought to everything. In her kitchen, Rebecca created something beyond food; she crafted experiences, each dish a new surprise that felt personal and alive. For the first time, he felt a conflict between ambition and desire.

When Joseph Cashin, Rebecca's father, brought his business to the firm as one of Wales' new accounts, he saw the relationship as a positive move up. His visits to Joseph's home to deliver paperwork on behalf of the firm were good, too. Rebecca was there providing interesting conversations along with her treats. His favorite was her apple pie.

Wales felt disillusioned after the incident on the street. He hoped for a simple visit with Alice, but this wasn't to be. He intended to talk to her about marriage and their future. Rebecca's meddling threw everything into disarray and left him questioning his actions. Why was he so indecisive? He could fake confidence but feel it. No.

As the cab navigated the streets of New York, his frustration simmered. Amidst the disarray of the city, he yearned for something credible, something that resonated with the person he truly was. *Everyone is so consumed with their own agendas, their own facades. Is this really the life I want?*

*　　*　　*

Wales felt a pang of nostalgia. It was a year since he'd earned his position at Bidwell & Strong, the most prestigious law firm in New York. Surrounded by the success he dreamed of, and a life far removed from his upbringing, he couldn't shake the sense of dissatisfaction.

Wasn't this what I wanted? To join a reputable law firm, rise through the ranks, secure success? Marry a wealthy daughter and settle into a life of ease? His footsteps echoed through the marble-clad lobby as he climbed the grand staircase to his office.

As he took in the ornate furnishings and polished surfaces, bitterness crossed his mind: This place… it's nothing but a gilded cage. *What was the point of all this success*, he wondered, *if it meant sacrificing reality?*

Reaching his small, windowless office on the third floor, a wave of frustration hit Wales. Everything here felt so contrived, so stifling; he yearned for a place where he could be himself, free from judgment or pretense.

I can't keep pretending, he resolved, sinking into his leather desk chair with a heavy sigh. *There must be more to life than this.*

Where could he find it?

Amidst the turmoil, a faint flicker of hope ignited. *What if I dared to take a chance on something different?*

Then a fleeting impression flashed through his mind. Rebecca's smile when she was in quiet reflection or the light reflecting on her red hair. *What if I convinced Rebecca to go with me?*

Wait, no! What am I thinking? Alice is the one I need to court. Wales shook his head. *Besides, Rebecca is the last one I should think about.*

As he sat in his office, Wales dwelt on the emptiness of his personal life. Aside from his brother in Queens, he had no real family. Even the sibling bond had frayed over the years, their relationship nearly severed in the aftermath of their father's death.

In the early days, they had been inseparable, leaning on each other through the hardships of their upbringing. But as Wales pursued his ambitions, the distance between them grew.

His brother had chosen a quieter, simpler life, one that Wales had once admired but later dismissed in his pursuit of success. Their last exchange—a short, stilted letter—was now a faded memory, the words barely recalling the closeness they once shared.

Maybe he was right to pull away, Wales considered, bitterness creeping in. Yet beneath the resentment lay something else, a longing for the connection he'd lost.

*   *   *

William Darcy then sauntered into Wales' office. His presence shattered the silence heralded by the overpowering scent of his cologne. "Well, what happened, old chap?" he asked, his tone laced with eager anticipation. "Did you finally muster the courage to ask Alice for her hand in marriage?"

Wales hesitated, Darcy's enthusiasm striking a sour note in him. He recalled Rebecca's cryptic warning, a subtle hint that had cast a shadow over his trust in his friend. "Um... not yet," he forced a smile. "The timing didn't seem quite right."

Darcy let out a disappointed sigh. "Oh, come now! You've had ages to figure this out." Wales nodded, unsure of how to reconcile the friend he once knew with the doubts now clouding his mind.

Darcy waved off Wales's hesitation with characteristic nonchalance. "No worries, mate. Tomorrow's another day. Keep the ladies on their toes, I say. It's all part of the game," he declared with a grin.

"Right... sure," Wales mind still consumed by his departure. "Anyway, I've got a stack of cases to tackle. How about dinner tomorrow?"

"Absolutely! I've got plans for a charming young lady tonight. I'll see if she has a friend to join us," Darcy replied, already moving away.

As Darcy's echoing footsteps on the marble floor faded into the distance, Wales found himself enveloped once more by the silence. Leaning forward, he rested his head in his hand, the weight of his own indecision bearing down upon him.

Rebecca's presence still loomed large. Alongside the flicker of attraction, uncertainty burned — was it passion that stirred within him, or the fear of the unknown? She both excited and terrified him.

Rebecca, Alice, and other women who crossed his path were mere catalysts for this awakening, mirrors reflecting to him the emptiness. Wales realized he could not attribute these feelings to any one person; they emanated from a place within himself.

*   *   *

That evening, as Wales settled into his modest bachelor apartment, he sank into the well-worn armchair left behind by a previous tenant. It creaked under his weight, its cushions bearing the imprint of years, but it was familiar, comfortable.

Wales let out a sigh, the tension in his shoulders easing as he shrugged off his restrictive jacket and tossed it onto the floor. With a quick tug, he loosened his collar, breathing freely for the first time that day. Here, at least, he could let down his guard, if only for a few fleeting hours.

He let his mind drift.

In the quiet, Wales could almost hear his maid, Nancy, fussing over his scattered attire—a familiar admonishment that had grown oddly comforting. Nancy's dedication to maintaining order in his otherwise unremarkable apartment was unwavering. She straightened his discarded jackets, ironed his handkerchiefs, organized his papers, and occasionally left a warm meal waiting for him. Despite his half-hearted protests, she treated his space as if it were a haven worth preserving.

But beyond her attentive care, Nancy was one of the few people who seemed interested in his life. She'd ask him questions that no one else bothered to—small, thoughtful inquiries about his day, his well-being, his family. Though she scolded him for his messiness, he compensated her well, grateful not only for her work, but for her presence.

With a sense of anticipation, Wales reached for the familiar comfort of the *New York Tribune*, placed by Nancy alongside his armchair. The newspaper, filled with tales of daring exploits, far-flung discoveries, and the latest headlines, was a small luxury that offered him an escape from his regimented routine.

Here he could lose himself in the excitement of explorers and adventurers—a temporary reprieve from the life he was questioning with each passing day.

As he perused the pages, his eyes alighted upon a discovery, causing his hands to tremble in surprise. Was it a coincidence, or a twist of fate orchestrated by God? An advertisement nestled within the folds of the newspaper beckoned to him with its promise of adventure.

"Lawyers Wanted—Growing Frontier Town Seeks Legal Help," the headline proclaimed, capturing Wales's attention with an almost magnetic pull.

He leaned in, delving into the details of the article, which painted a vivid picture of Belvidere, Illinois—a burgeoning town on the edge of the Midwestern prairie, transformed by the addition of a new train depot. It was a place of raw opportunity, its population growing by the day as settlers arrived with dreams of carving out a future.

The town, it seemed, needed someone with his skills, someone who could navigate the legal needs of a community in flux. It needed stability, guidance—a chance for him to be more than just another name in the New York directories.

As he pondered the possibilities, a flicker of excitement stirred within him, growing with each line he reread. Could this be the opportunity he had been searching for, the chance to escape the hollow rituals and suffocating expectations of New York society?

Wales read the advertisement for the umpteenth time, his mind racing with visions of a new life. A fresh start, far from the endless climb up the social ladder, a place where he could make a real impact. A surge of excitement climbed through his veins.

"I must seize this moment," he whispered to himself with newfound conviction, as anticipation surged through him, bright and undeniable. Tomorrow, he would leave behind the comfort—and the constraints—of everything he'd known. Put aside the Wales W. Wood, who struggled with confidence and embraced something new.

Without hesitation, Wales planned his departure. Flipping to the back of the *Tribune*, he found the train schedule and noted the noon departure for Chicago. He would be on that train, bound for the West.

Fueled by urgency, Wales rummaged through his drawers, gathering the essentials and packing them into a worn carpetbag. Two suits would suffice, he decided, feeling a quiet thrill at leaving behind the strict dress codes and pretenses of New York's elite. He would trade them in for the simplicity of the open frontier.

At his small, well-used desk, Wales poised a quill over a blank sheet of parchment. He penned his resignation from Bidwell & Strong, a final farewell to the firm that had tethered him to a life of stifling conformity. As he composed his words, a weight lifted from his shoulders, replaced by a sense of exhilaration at the unknown life waiting for him. Folding the letter into an envelope, he resolved to send it via messenger first thing in the morning.

With his affairs in order and his path clear, one task remained—he would withdraw his savings from the bank, purchase a one-way ticket to Chicago, and then onward to Belvidere. A new chapter lay before him, untouched by the shadows of his past. Tomorrow, New York would fade into the distance as he embraced the promise of an untamed future.

Finally, as he lay down on his lumpy old mattress for one last night, he dreamed not of ornate rooms or polished offices, but of open skies and nights spent beneath the stars.

*   *   *

With a sense of purpose driving him forward, Wales set his plans into motion swiftly the next morning. Fueled by adrenaline, he selected his attire with care—a sturdy pair of pants, a simple button-up shirt, and his most comfortable boots. A vest with handkerchiefs, a light jacket, and his hat completed the ensemble, balancing practicality with comfort for the journey ahead.

He continued to pack his carpetbag with essentials—toiletries, his best razor, and a small bottle of cologne to combat any travel odors—Wales wasted no time on sentimentality. He intended to buy breakfast from a street vendor, eager to get moving.

With a decisive flick of his wrist, he tossed yesterday's newspaper onto the floor as he made room on the table to pen a brief note to Nancy. In straightforward terms, he apologized for his abrupt departure and instructed her to sell his belongings to settle any remaining debts. The room, paid for until month's end, would give her time to manage things.

Today marked the start of a new chapter—one brimming with uncertainty but rich with promise. As Wales stepped into the bustling New York streets, anticipation coursed through his veins. There were no second glances, no lingering attachments; he was resolute in leaving it all behind.

At the City Bank, he withdrew his entire savings, claiming the funds were for a transfer to another office. After dispatching his resignation to Bidwell & Strong, he was sure he had made a clean break from his former life.

With a substantial sum of money on him, Wales, wary of thieves, slipped into a secluded corner to hide the funds in various pockets and compartments. The fear of losing all he had was unsettling, but this way, at least part of his cash might remain safe if misfortune struck.

His preparations complete, Wales made his way to the train station. The ticket agent raised an eyebrow when Wales requested a one-way ticket to Chicago, curiosity flickering in his gaze.

"Leaving everything behind, eh, son?" The agent sized him up with mild interest.

Wales nodded, resolve unwavering. "I need a fresh start," his words heavy with the weight of his decision. "The city has lost its appeal."

The agent gave him a knowing nod as Wales accepted his ticket and tucked it safely into his jacket pocket, a tangible promise for his new journey.

Boarding the train, Wales found a solitary window seat, his heart pounding as the locomotive chugged to life, pulling him away from the crowded streets and into the unknown. For the first time in years, Wales felt unburdened.

Yet as the train rattled westward, he could not shake thoughts of Rebecca Cashin. The tension between them, her cryptic warnings—they lingered like an unhealed wound. But despite his emotions, he knew this was a journey of his own, filled with promise, possibility, and the alluring mystery of the unknown.

*   *   *

Wales stirred from one of his many naps, the hazy edges of sleep still clinging to his mind as he registered the low voices intruding upon his solitude. He did not expect long periods of boredom on this long journey west, and usually, no one lingered at the back of his favorite train car. Blinking groggily, he strained to make sense of the conversation unfolding nearby.

"Sir, you do not know who you're dealing with," one voice insisted, its tone edged with menace. "The Pinkerton Agency will not be pleased. It is best you put aside your weapon."

Wales's heart quickened as the words sank in. Still half-awake, he struggled to comprehend the reality of the situation. *Weapon? This must be a misunderstanding—I do not have a weapon.*

Then another voice, deeper and more measured, sliced through the tension. "Alright, I do

not want to attract attention, but you owe me. The…
Volunteers… are not as generous as I am."

Wales tensed as he felt the seat beside him shift, his senses sharpening despite his efforts to keep up the pretense of sleep. Who were these men, and why were they speaking so close to him?

The first man, rattled, shifted his tone. "Of course, of course. I always reward decent work, but I have nothing on me at the moment, and we wouldn't want to… disturb… my friend here. He has got quite the aim, you know."

A shiver ran down Wales's spine as he realized they were now implicating him in their exchange. His mind raced, his pulse quickening. *Who are these men, and what do they want from me?*

"We'll meet in Chicago, then," the deeper voice declared, footsteps retreating toward the forward car.

As the train rattled onward, Wales's mind buzzed with questions. He resolved to remain vigilant, uncertain of what other surprises lay in wait.

A moment later, the stranger beside him leaned back, chuckling. Wales opened his eyes and sat up slowly, offering a wry smile. "Rarely a sleeping man plays a part in such drama," he remarked, voice laced with amusement.

The man beside him laughed, his eyes sparkling with mischief. "Ah, so you *were* awake! You played the part well. Our friend back there is not a mastermind—too afraid to take risks. I have known that about him for years, so I made the best of what I had." He extended his hand. "Thomas Humphrey, at your service."

"Wales W. Wood, late of New York City," He replied, Thomas's hand.

"Not affiliated with the National Volunteers, I hope?" Thomas asked, his gaze sharpened. "They are wrapped up in some rather unsavory business. That character you just 'protected' is one of their ranks."

Wales shook his head. "No, nothing like that. I am a lawyer, trained in Albany. I am heading west to Belvidere, looking for…" he paused, struggling to find the words, "something new."

Thomas gave him a knowing look. "Let me guess—you need a change of scenery. Some woman back East did not take kindly to you?"

"No, nothing like that," Wales said, chuckling despite himself. "Society games. People playing me for a fool. And the firm… well, it just felt like a box I could not escape from. I could not breathe."

Thomas nodded, listening. A sense of camaraderie bloomed between them as the conversation unfolded.

"You know," Thomas mused, gazing past Wales out the window, "intrigue is in my blood. My grandfather fought in the Revolution, and my father served in the War of 1812. There is a growing divide in this country, Wales. We must keep the Union strong."

Wales nodded, admiration creeping into his voice. "You speak as someone who understands the importance of choosing one's battles carefully," he observed. "I'm a Union man myself, though I'm not sure how to serve it best."

Thomas leaned in, his voice dropping to a conspiratorial whisper. "What if I told you there's a way to satisfy that desire for adventure while also serving the Union?"

Wales raised an eyebrow, intrigued.

"My company, the Pinkerton National Detective Agency, is expanding westward. We are gathering intelligence on extremist factions that threaten the Union's stability. We need someone discreet, with your skills, to be our eyes and ears in Belvidere."

A flicker of excitement sparked in Wales's chest, though he kept his expression measured. "It's tempting. But why trust me? We have just met."

Thomas's smile turned wry. "Intuition. Call it a soldier's instinct, honed over years of knowing who to trust. And" he added, "I've already seen you manage a tense situation with grace." He gestured toward the empty seat where their disgruntled fellow passenger had been. "You played along without a blink. That is the quick thinking we need."

Wales's pulse quickened as Thomas laid out the plan. Here was an opportunity to embark on a grand adventure but also contribute to a cause greater than himself.

"You see, we already have agents in Richmond," Thomas continued, "and now it is time to fortify our presence in the west. And I think we have just found our man. If you can be discreet."

Wales met Thomas's gaze, his voice steady with determination. "If it means helping protect the Union, you can count me in."

Thomas's face lit up with enthusiasm. "Then you will be my man in Belvidere. But first, I will need to ensure you fit the Pinkerton profile, just in case anyone asks. Are you a drinker, by chance? Smoke, play cards, visit lowly places, swear a bit?"

Wales frowned, puzzled. "That seems specific. Why does it matter?"

"Pinkerton has his standards," Thomas explained with a grin. "We need men who can be trusted, especially if we're trusting them to lie."

Wales smirked, shaking his head. "Strange that an agency built on deception values trust above all. But, for the record, I do not drink, cannot stand to smoke, am terrible at cards, and have no taste for lowly places. As for swearing... well, occasionally."

Thomas laughed, clapping him on the shoulder. "Perfect! You will fit in fine. The job's straightforward—send reports to our Chicago office about any suspicious goings-on in Belvidere. We will set you up with a code system for your telegraphs once you're settled in town. And since you will be practicing law, no one will think twice about messages going back and forth."

A thrill coursed through Wales as the reality of his new role sank in. This was the adventure he had been seeking—a chance to be effective and find himself anew.

"Mr. Humphrey, when I left New York, I wanted adventure," he marveled, still processing the twist of fate that had led him here.

"It keeps you alive, Wales. It is time to live!" Thomas said, sealing their pact with a firm handshake as the train thundered westward.

For Wales, this was the beginning.

Chapter Three

Rebecca stood on the bustling street seething as memories of Wales's sudden disappearance resurfaced. Her face flushed with anger, and as she muttered under her breath, passersby cast quick, sidelong glances, unwilling to witness her humiliation or engage with her fury.

"How dare he!" she hissed, clenching her fists and slamming the package in her hand to the ground. The sting of his rejection cut deeply. She had tried to move on, but the memory of their almost kiss lingered like an unhealed wound, leaving her to question if it had ever been real.

A horse's neigh jolted her back to the present. The delivery man stared at her, annoyed. "Miss, I do not care who you are. You are paying for that bundle of carrots you tossed in the dirt. Are you going to sign for this or not? I have other places to be today," he snapped.

"Oh, yes, of course. I am… I am sorry," she stammered, handing him a few coins and signing the bill.

"Thank you, miss," he replied as Rebecca picked the dusty carrots, adding them to the other vegetables waiting on the doorstep until Jenny whisked them into the house.

She forced herself to focus on the task at hand, but no matter how she tried, she could not shake Wales or the sting of his parting words. She made her way to the kitchen, still carrying the lingering ache of his absence.

It was then she noticed it—a handkerchief she had tucked away in the kitchen drawer, one she hadn't been able to part with.

Wales's handkerchief.

She pulled it out, opened the top grading of the stove, and held it over the smoldering embers below, her hand trembling as she considered letting the flames consume this last piece of his memory.

Her face hardened as she whispered to herself, "If he can disappear so easily, why should I hold on to this?"

But just as her fingers loosened, ready to let it drop, she hesitated. Memories surged unbidden— their almost kiss, the way he had looked at her with a mix of challenge and vulnerability, the warmth in his voice when he'd shared his ambitions. His departure, though sharp, was not the whole story.

With a frustrated sigh, she drew her hand back and folded the handkerchief, tucking it away in the small compartment of her jewelry box in her bedroom. She slammed the lid shut, as if locking away that piece of him—and the ache it brought.

"Fine," she murmured. "I will keep it. For now."

Yet as she returned to her work, she could understand Wales or the mystery of his disappearance. She had tried to locate him within weeks of his leaving, asking around his apartment and even questioning mutual acquaintances. But her efforts yielded nothing.

"Where could he have gone?" she wondered aloud, frustration clear in her voice. The mystery consumed her and longing for a resolution that seemed out of reach.

*   *   *

"There's a change in the air." Rebecca Cashin silently observed. The influx of gentlemen clad in blue military uniforms around town resulted from the Confederate attack on Fort Sumter in South Carolina. The war between the states had begun.

"New York is doing its part!" her father announced as he swept into the house, placing his hat on the rack before settling at the kitchen table. "Thirty regiments formed the day after the attack and siege on the fort. I have a team at the factory figuring out how we might secure a contract with the Federals. Your new brother-in-law can lend a hand to the family."

Rebecca nodded, focusing on her baking. She was experimenting with cinnamon; a spice the market vendor had suggested she try. It was warm, inviting aroma wafted through the kitchen, drawing her father in, who now awaited the first taste. Jenny, who shared her appreciation for the finer results of Rebecca's baking, kept their new "Good Stove" from the Troy Stove Works well-stocked with coal.

"My dear, it smells divine!" her father exclaimed, leaning in.

"Yes, it has a nice aroma," she replied, distracted. "The vendor advised just a touch in the sweetbread, with a sprinkle of sugar on top while it's warm."

Rebecca opened the oven door, smiling as she saw the loaf browned to perfection. She pulled it from the stove and carried it over to the table, half-listening to her father, who continued chatting.

"Oh, and even better news, Rebecca," he said, his tone carrying a certain satisfaction. "You don't have to worry about that Wales fellow bothering you any longer."

"What?" Rebecca nearly dropped the bread, placing it down on the table, her heart pounding at the unexpected mention of his name. Regaining her composure, she replied, "I mean…um… tell."

Her father did not notice her reaction and went on, "My friend at the firm told me Mr. Wales—that deceiver—sent a resignation letter with no notice a few months back. Just up and left. Abandoned his job at the firm without a word. Poor professional decision on the lad's part. He has sacrificed his entire career, I imagine. Makes me wonder if he took advantage of some poor girl and skipped town."

She watched as her father cut a slice of the sweetbread, took a contented bite, and settled back in his chair, savoring it. Meanwhile, her mind whirled. *Why hadn't he told her he was leaving? Why no letter, no explanation? Could there have been another woman?*

She felt a pang of resentment at his sudden, unexplained disappearance. She could not blame him for wanting a change, given the pressure he had been under, but his abruptness left her feeling… abandoned.

"Time to set your sights on a new man," her father continued, oblivious to her inner turmoil. "Someone more suitable. Not a lawyer this time, hmm? What about a doctor or a politician? Surely there must be a man in this city who is right for you." He chuckled, cutting another slice of bread.

In truth, she could not shake the connection she felt to Wales, even now, and the tension that had lingered between them. There was a mystery to his sudden disappearance that haunted her. Part of her yearned for closure, but another part wondered if there was more to his story—a truth that might explain everything.

I must find him, her brow creased. *But where do I begin?*

*   *   *

Two years later, Rebecca found herself at yet another social gathering, this time in the arm of Mr. George Ellington—a competent doctor but, as she had discovered, dull company. Though technically her escort, George had wandered off earlier in the evening, and she had been searching for him ever since. She spotted him in the back garden with Miss Margaret Milestone.

He isn't as dull as I thought, she mused.

Resigned, Rebecca drifted back to the parlor and found herself amid normal gossip with the other ladies. But her heart skipped a beat when she overheard a familiar name spoken nearby— "Wales Wood." She scanned the crowd and locked eyes with Mr. William Darcy, one of Wales's former colleagues at Bidwell & Strong. Now a partner at the firm, Darcy was as notorious for his charm as for his reputation as a rake.

Of all people. Suppressing a sigh. *Best to get it over with.*

She maneuvered her way closer to Darcy's circle, feigning interest as she caught snippets of the conversation.

"Can you believe Wales wants me to leave New York and join him in Belvidere, Illinois? Has he lost his mind?" Darcy exclaimed to the group, his tone a mix of disbelief and disdain. The War of the Rebellion showed no sign of ending, and Wales was out west.

Rebecca's pulse quickened. Could it be Wales Wood he was talking about? Her heart raced as she listened, the thrill of finding a clue after years of wondering and searching overwhelming her.

"He's out there, surrounded by the Federal Army," Darcy continued, raising a fist in frustration.

"Where they're calling for more soldiers to fight those damn rebels."

Darcy glanced over and noticed her interest, flashing her a charming smile as he continued to bemoan Wales's departure and his own reluctance to follow. Rebecca returned his smile, masking her impatience. Feeding his ego was easy enough, but she could not contain her curiosity any longer.

"Excuse me, Mr. Darcy," Rebecca interjected, her voice trembling. "Did I hear correctly? Did you say Wales Wood went to Illinois?"

Darcy turned to her, ready to lay on his charm. "Ah, Miss Cashin, yes, he did indeed. A dreadful backwater town called Belvidere. He has been begging me to join him there and start a law firm." He smirked. "Chicago but Belvidere? No, thank you."

Rebecca's mind whirled with disbelief and excitement. She had found him! She pressed for more information, doing her best to appear casual. "But why Illinois? What could have taken him there?"

Darcy sighed, shaking his head. "Honestly, I have no idea. He wrote to me months ago, inviting me to join him. But I am a partner at Bidwell & Strong now. Why would I leave New York? I paid handsomely to keep my place here rather than risk life and limb in a muddy camp." Darcy shuddered. "The blood, the bullets, the horrid conditions—can you imagine?"

Rebecca fought to keep her expression composed, though irritation sparked in her chest. "Indeed, it's quite surprising he'd ask that of you," she replied, nodding sympathetically. "Thank you, Mr. Darcy, for enlightening me."

He nodded, pleased with her attention. "No problem, my dear. And Miss Cashin, tell me, what are your plans for the evening? Your father made quite a lucrative deal with the United States Government, I hear…"

Of course he would know, resisting the urge to roll her eyes. Plastering on a polite smile, she replied, "Another time, Mr. Darcy. Thank you."

She walked away before he could press further, slipping out the front door without a second thought for Mr. Ellington or any of the others. She hailed a cab, her mind buzzing with possibility. *Belvidere.* She had found a trace of him.

As the carriage trundled home, her plans turned inward. She could not deny her curiosity—the need to know why Wales had vanished so suddenly without a word to her. Was she the reason he had left?

Had he lost interest? Or was there someone else? Frustration surged, but beneath it lay something deeper: a longing she could no longer ignore.

I know what I am thinking is impulsive, she realized. *If he wants nothing to do with me, he can tell me to my face.* She knew a journey like this would be risky, even reckless, but she could not let the mystery—and the ache—continue to haunt her.

As her home came into view, she took a steadying breath. She would go to Belvidere, whatever it took, to find Wales Wood. To confront him and lay her questions to rest.

*   *   *

Gathering her courage, Rebecca planned her next move. Once home, she busied herself in the kitchen, preparing a loaf of sweet bread with bits of chocolate folded into the dough. As she waited for it to bake, she rehearsed the story she would tell her father.

When the loaf finished and resting on the kitchen table, she heard the front door open and her father's familiar call, "I'm home!"

"In the kitchen!" she answered, smiling as the door creaked open. Joseph Cashin entered, his eyes lighting up at the sight of the warm loaf, and Rebecca felt her confidence strengthen—until her sister, Emily, swept in behind him, her presence both unexpected and unwelcome. Emily's gaze fell on her and the bread with a look of thinly veiled curiosity and disdain.

Their father's surprise was clear. "Rebecca, it smells wonderful! What is the occasion?"

Rebecca ignored Emily and pulled up a chair, inviting her father to do the same. "Father, may I visit a friend in Chicago? Do you remember Miss Kattie Sprinkle? She traveled there with her father." This part was true, though the rest of her story was a fabrication she would soon clarify with a letter to Kattie.

Rebecca continued, "Kattie wrote to say she is recovering from a recent illness, something like the grippe, and she mentioned she's craving company. Since things have been quiet here, I thought I might join her."

Emily chuckled, a sly grin spreading across her face. "Chicago, is it? How convenient. Tell me, Rebecca, is there someone about whom we do not know? A suitor, perhaps? We all know you have little interest in the men here in New York—given how many you have turned down."

Rebecca's cheeks flushed with indignation, but she held her tongue, knowing any protest would fuel Emily's curiosity and spite.

Joseph Cashin furrowed his brow. "It's good to help a friend," he said, dismissing Emily's jibe with a wave of his hand. "Not everything is about suitors, Emily. But who knows? Kattie's father is well-connected in Chicago with the railroad men. If Rebecca were to make a fine acquaintance while she is there, all the better."

Emily's laugh cut sharply through the room. "Of course, Father. How noble of Rebecca to come to the rescue. But forgive me if I find her sudden 'altruism' a bit… convenient. She is leaving something out."

Rebecca clenched her fists, struggling to keep her composure. "I assure you, Emily, this is not a frivolous endeavor."

Their father interjected, his voice firm. "Enough, both of you. Rebecca, you are free to go if this is something you wish to do. But promise you will keep me informed of your whereabouts and take every precaution to stay safe."

Rebecca met her father's gaze, gratitude swelling in her chest despite Emily's antagonism. "Thank you, Father. I will write often, I promise."

Her father's expression softened, though a trace of concern lingered. "One more thing, Rebecca," he said, setting down his slice of bread and meeting her eyes with a serious look. "While you are away, I want you to use your head. Do not let yourself be swept up by some Union soldier looking to play the hero. A man in uniform might seem thrilling, but a soldier's life is dangerous, especially in times like these."

He leaned forward, his voice low and earnest. "We both know what it would mean for this family if you married well to someone established and secure. A soldier could easily go off and die, leaving you with nothing but an uncertain future. I want your life to be stable and successful, Rebecca, as would your mother."

Rebecca nodded, doing her best to appear reassured. "Of course, Father," she replied with a small smile.

Emily rolled her eyes, lifting her hand to hide her smirk. "Father's right, Rebecca," she added with mock sincerity. "We wouldn't want you to end up widowed before you've even had a real chance at society."

Rebecca shot her sister a look but maintained her composure. Her father's words echoed in her mind, but they did not dampen her resolve. She was not going to Chicago to be swept off her feet—she was going to find Wales and uncover the truth.

*   *   *

When the train pulled into Belvidere, Illinois, a few weeks later, Rebecca's heart sank. The town was quite different from the bustling streets of New York or even the vibrant energy of Chicago. It felt disappointingly small and unremarkable after all the effort she had put into getting there.

She had packed lightly, expecting to find a dress shop in town, and securing the second ticket from Chicago to Belvidere on the Galena and Chicago Union Railroad had been easy. She had even promised herself that if her trip proved pointless, she would return to Chicago and stay with Kattie Sprinkle and her family.

As the train doors opened with a creak, Rebecca stepped onto the dusty platform, squinting against the late afternoon sun. The only nearby sounds were the locomotive's whistle and the shuffle of her footsteps on the worn wooden boards. In the distance, near the town center, she saw a crowd and heard occasional bursts of cheering.

What is going on over there? she wondered, scanning her surroundings.

The station attendant glanced up from his newspaper, eyeing her with mild curiosity. "Afternoon, miss. Bit of a long journey from Chicago for just one passenger. Are you expecting someone in Belvidere? Here to see your man off to fight? Had young ladies come through yesterday for the same reason."

See him off to fight? The words jolted her, but she kept her expression polite and steady. "Yes… I am here to see him off," she replied, her heart beating faster. "His name is Wood—Mr. Wales Wood. Do you know him?"

The white-haired attendant nodded. "I sure do! Good man, that one. Up-and-coming lawyer. He has helped folks secure land for their own. He's Lieutenant of our own 95th Illinois Regiment, about to head to the front. He is likely in the town square with the others."

Rebecca's heart skipped. *Lieutenant of the 95th?* She had not expected him to be so directly involved. She was both proud and anxious.

The attendant pointed down the road. "See that hotel across the street? That is where the respectable women stay. Best spot for a young lady like yourself while you are here in town. Safer than the rooms over the saloon." With that, he returned to his reading, leaving Rebecca to herself.

"Thank you," she murmured, clutching her carpetbag. She crossed the street to the hotel, a modest building that was nothing like the ones back home. Still, she came too far to turn back now. After securing a room toward the back, she dropped off her things and freshened up.

She returned to the town square, taking in the scene with sharp eyes. It was alive with activity, filled with recruits, their families, and townsfolk there to see them off. Young men, barely more than boys, lined up with faces pinched. Among them were older men with weathered faces, ready to lend their experience to the cause, and even a line of women volunteering as nurses, the only role the Union allowed them to take on since last year.

The air is alive with patriotic fervor, Rebecca observed. She felt an unexpected thrill—it was rare for her to feel moved by such passion. If she could speak to Wales, he would want her to stay and help. And if he did, she would join him, whatever it took.

If he has feelings for me as I do for him, then there is no reason to rush back home.

She maneuvered through the bustling crowd toward the square, hoping to spot Wales. If he was not there, she was determined to search every corner of Belvidere until she found him. Nurses in their dark uniforms gathered nearby, the men gave them respectful nods; Rebecca knew these women would provide care and comfort on the battlefield.

Her gaze shifted to the line of nurses. *They will be there,* she realized, her eyes narrowed. *If they can go, why can't I?* She approached the line, entertaining the idea of joining them.

But a tall, broad-shouldered woman with her hair pulled back in a severe white bun intercepted her. She wore a stained apron that bore signs of the battlefield. "Sorry, miss," the woman said, looking Rebecca up and down with a dismissive glance. "We are full up. Besides, that pretty dress will not stay so nice out there. High-class ladies like you do not last long. Kiss your man goodbye, and we will take care of him on the battlefield. Go on now."

The blunt dismissal left Rebecca stunned. Instead of discouragement, however, indignation and defiance flared within her. *Who is this woman to decide what I am capable of?*

Looking around, she took in the young recruits—many of whom looked scarcely old enough to shave, let alone march into battle. A spark of inspiration struck. *If they can enlist, then why can't I?* A disguise, a quick change in appearance, and she could blend in. The idea was both thrilling and terrifying.

If Wales is going to war, then I will not be left behind, she resolved. *If I cannot join as a nurse, I'll find another way.*

With a deep breath, Rebecca steeled herself, a new determination burning within her. She would reach Wales, no matter what it took.

*　　*　　*

Rebecca's hands trembled as she stood in front of the mirror. The trousers and shirt—plain and nondescript—were easy enough to put on, but it was the Marseilles vest that solidified her transformation. She slid it over her shoulders, fastening it, feeling the padded material press against her chest. The vest was not just for appearances; it was her armor.

Her breath quickened as she tugged at the vest, hiding her feminine curves and offering a practical solution for the monthly inconveniences she would have to manage in secret. The padding, designed to mimic a man's muscle, provided her with the cover she needed. A single slip, one wrong move, and her life could be over. This was not just deception—it was survival.

Holding the knife she stole from the hotel kitchen steady; Rebecca raised it to her hair. She sliced through the dark red strands in deliberate strokes, watching them fall to the floor, remnants of the life she was leaving behind. Her heart pounded as she cut, each snip took her a step further away from the girl she had been.

When she finished, she pulled a straw hat low over her brow and studied her reflection. The woman she had known all her life was gone, replaced by a stranger—a young man. She took a deep, steadying breath, whispering to herself, "Not too bad," evaluating her voice as she dropped it into a low rumble she had practiced in private. Straightening her posture, she felt the tension in her shoulders ease. There could be no hesitation, no slip-ups. If she kept her cap low and her shirt loose, no one would see through her disguise.

With her heart pounding, she slipped out the hotel's back door and into the cool afternoon air. Her feet moved of their own accord, carrying her closer to the town square and the line of recruits. Cheers and shouts echoed through the street as she approached, each step feeling like another nail in her coffin. She had come here to find Wales, but now her journey was something much larger—a dangerous game she was beginning to understand.

The square buzzed with excitement as boys lined up to join the 95th Illinois Regiment. There was an electric energy in the crowd—fear mixed with a thrill of adventure—and Rebecca felt it coursing through her, steadying her nerves even as her heart raced.

As she joined the line of recruits, a wave of anxiety washed over her. What if someone recognized her? What if the officers saw through her disguise? She could feel her hands growing cold, her heartbeat thundering in her ears. Men crowded in around her, their bodies pressing close, and each accidental brush against her heightened her fear of discovery.

"Oi! You there!" a voice rang out behind her, sharp and accusing. Her blood ran cold, and for a split second, her heart had stopped. Panic gripped her as she scanned for an escape route.

But before she could react, a gangly young man beside her nudged her arm and grinned. "You are up next, mate! Line's moving," he said, nodding toward the enlistment table up ahead. "I am Samuel Pepper. Sam for short. Who might you be?"

The world circled again, and Rebecca forced herself to breathe. She had practiced this lie, but now, under pressure, it felt foreign on her tongue. "Albert… Albert Cashin," she replied gruffly, praying the name sounded convincing.

Samuel clapped her on the shoulder. "Good to meet ya, Albert! We are all in this together, eh? Let us get it over with—I've got some girls to kiss before we leave tomorrow."

The line shuffled forward, and Rebecca moved with it, her legs feeling like lead. At the enlistment table, officers sat with quills poised, casting their eyes over each recruit as they signed. One officer's gaze lingered on her a moment too long, and her breath caught. Her pulse raced as she forced herself to stand still, hoping her disguise held.

Finally, the officer gestured toward the quill, his voice weary. "Name and residence."

Relief flooded through her, making her knees buckle. She grabbed the quill, her hand trembling as she scrawled her false name on the parchment: Albert Cashin. With each stroke, she felt her old identity slipping away, replaced by the stranger she'd become.

As she handed the form back, she heard a familiar voice nearby, and her heart skipped a beat.

"Lieutenant Wood, a moment, please."

Rebecca's head snapped up just in time to see him. Wales Wood, dressed in the crisp blue coat of the Federal Army, moved through the crowd with an air of authority. His face was sharper, more focused than she remembered, and as he gathered a stack of enlistment forms from the table, he walked right past her, mere feet away. He was so close she could have reached out to touch him. Her breath caught, and she froze, torn between the urge to call out and the need to remain hidden.

"Make way," someone muttered, pulling her out of her daze. "That is Lieutenant Wales Wood. Do not want to piss him off."

Her pulse hammered as she watched him disappear into the crowd, oblivious to her presence. She had come so close, and yet he had not even noticed her. She could feel a tumult of emotions swirling within her, but there was no time to dwell on them.

"Well, Albert Cashin, from back east, eh?" Samuel grinned, nudging her again. "Ready to do your part?"

Rebecca swallowed, forcing herself to respond in the deep voice she'd practiced. "Right. Here to serve."

Samuel laughed, nudging her as the line moved again. "And that sixty dollars doesn't hurt, does it?"

But Rebecca barely heard him, still shaken by the sight of Wales so close, yet out of reach. Drawing a deep breath, she squared her shoulders. There would be time later to untangle the mess of emotions he stirred in her. Right now, she had to survive the next steps.

That night, alone in her rented room, Rebecca packed her gear. Tomorrow, they would board the train to Camp Fuller, and she would begin her journey as a soldier. Seeing Wales had shaken her more than she had expected—he was right there, leading men, preparing for battle. What if he noticed her again? What if he recognized her?

The next morning, the train depot was alive with farewells and last-minute promises. Rebecca kept her head down, slipping onto the train unnoticed. She found a seat at the back, pulling her hat low as the conductor's shout rang out. "All aboard!"

As the train jolted to life, pulling away from the station, Rebecca gazed out the window, watching Belvidere fade into the distance. She had escaped discovery today, but she knew the road ahead would grow more challenging. She was not just another soldier heading to war—she was a woman in hiding, her life hanging on the fragile success of her disguise.

Chapter Four

Wales Wood stared at his navy wool coat hanging on a peg at the entrance of his tent. The once-vibrant blue hue dulled by layers of dust from the journey to Camp Fuller, and the gold buttons, embossed with the fierce visage of an American eagle, seemed to catch the light as if to remind him of the duty he had taken on. It was quite different from the polished life he had left behind in New York.

He stepped out and surveyed the rows upon rows of standard-issue tents stretching across the encampment, their canvas sides flapping in the wind. The camp, meticulously arranged, was their home. Officers' tents, larger and positioned near the camp's center, marked the hub of command, while tents for enlistees, smaller and tightly clustered, stretched outward in neat rows, each company housed in its designated space.

Near the camp's edges were areas set aside for daily needs and tasks: mess tents where the smell of campfires and simple rations lingered, medical tents for the inevitable injuries, and storage spaces, where stacks of supplies were guarded. Latrines were placed far beyond the sleeping quarters, keeping the sanitary conditions in check—a necessity for soldiers unaccustomed to living in the elements.

As Wales took in the bustling camp, he saw men of all ranks adjusting to this new reality, soldiers who had once enjoyed the comforts of city life now learning to adapt to open skies, cold nights, and the rigid routines of army life. The camp was a world of its own, organized yet raw, with every row and regiment a reminder of the mission they had come here to serve.

They must be ready to live life rough. When we head south, they will learn to survive in the toughest conditions.

Once mustered, Wales poured over the *Revised Army Regulations and Tactics*, preparing himself for the realities of active service. They would remain stationed at Camp Fuller for weeks before departing Illinois, bound for the uncertain terrain of the rebel states.

During this time, the commissioned officers and enlistees grew accustomed to the demands of military life. They studied the theoretical aspects of warfare, practiced formations, and drilled daily, each man learning the duties of his rank. The camp bustled with instruction and discipline, transforming recent recruits into a cohesive fighting force.

An urgent call distracted Wales. "Lieutenant Wood! Your help if you please!" bellowed Colonel John Church from his tent.

Wales quickly rose, accustomed to these summonses as part of his role as Adjutant for the 95th Illinois Infantry. Managing dispatches, organizing meetings, and maintaining lines of communication fell squarely on his shoulders. Answering the Colonel's call marked yet another duty, but at least it came with certain privileges. He glanced around his tent, appreciating the private space with enough room to stand up in the center—a small but welcome luxury in camp life.

Nearby, Lieutenant Colonel Thomas Humphrey's tent stood beside Wales's, positioned close to the Colonel's tent as befit his rank. A short distance beyond lay the tent of Regimental Major Leander Bladen, with the other officers' tents extending along the ridge in descending order of rank. This careful arrangement reinforced the chain of command, each tent's placement signaling the hierarchy within the regiment.

This arrangement will not hold for long, Wales mused, glancing toward Humphrey's tent. *Thomas, as Lieutenant Colonel under Church, will not tolerate playing a secondary role to any man.* Wales knew Humphrey's ambitions well enough to sense the tension simmering just beneath the surface.

With a brisk "Yes, sir!" Wales grabbed his bag, packed with essentials: quill, paper, his field notebook, and a map. He hastened toward Colonel Church's tent, ready to take notes or relay any orders. Despite the Colonel's recent complaints of constant headaches, his knack for issuing commands showed no sign of fading.

Wales pulled back the tent flap, greeted by the heavy smell of liquor and sweat thickening the dim, stale air. Shadows cast by a flickering lantern fell across the pallor of Colonel Church's face, lending him an almost ghostly appearance. The sickbed seemed a far more fitting place than the rough confines of camp life.

Amidst his sense of duty, a seed of suspicion took root in Wales' mind. Despite Church's urgency, an unsettling feeling gnawed at him, whispering concealed motives. "What is it you need, sir?" Wales inquired, his tone a veneer of professionalism concealing his unease.

Reclining on a makeshift cot, Church gestured towards a rudimentary table and chair. "Draft a dispatch to Quarter Master Southworth," he commanded.

"Certainly, sir," Wales agreed, though his mind raced with questions.

"We need supplies for five hundred men to be requested as soon as he is ready. We have enough food donated for the moment, but it will not last forever." Church ordered. Wales understood the order and wrote it up as directed, but it was not correct. Almost a thousand men made up the 95th. Why the discrepancy in troop numbers?

"Sir, I think you might be inaccurate with the number of troops," Wales pointed out.

"Young man do not question my orders. I know how many soldiers we have. We have a surplus of supplies; we have donations from town coming in. We do not need so much." Colonel Church replied.

"Yes sir, but…" Wales wanted to explain the supplies were abundant for now. It would change when they started south in a few weeks, and they needed them then.

"Finish my request as stated, Lieutenant," said Church with an ice stare.

"Yes, sir," Wales responded, though a chill crept down his spine. He penned the dispatch and proffered it for review, but the Colonel glanced at it briefly before nodding. "Thank you, Wood. Send it off immediately," he murmured, dismissing Wales with a wave of his hand.

Outside, Wales nearly collided with Lieutenant Colonel Thomas Humphrey, who appeared equally troubled. "Wales, what did Church have you write?" Humphrey asked in a low tone.

Wales recounted the Colonel's orders, his voice filled with apprehension. "He is deceiving the Quartermaster, requesting supplies for five hundred men when our regiment has twice that. If we rely on those provisions, our recruits could starve before we even reach Tennessee."

Thomas's expression darkened. "I have been watching Church closely, Wales. There is something more to his condition. I suspect," he said with a quiet intensity, "that he may be a Confederate spy, planted to undermine our efforts. His behavior points to sabotage."

A shiver ran down Wales's spine as he absorbed this possibility. An enemy operative within their ranks left him uneasy. "But how can, you be sure?" he whispered, his tone betraying his fear.

Thomas scanned their surroundings before leaning closer. "We will need to watch him and gather evidence. This order could disrupt our entire supply line. There's treachery here, and we must uncover it. Have you spoken with the man managing the commissary wagon? He might know if Church has compromised anything else."

"No, I have not. Who oversees supplies?" asked Wales.

"John Scobell, a free Black man from Mississippi," replied Thomas, a hint of a smile touching his lips. "He is a civilian contractor, technically, but one of our most trusted hands—our cousin, in fact. Aunt Todd has many sons, as you know," Thomas added with a wink.

"Indeed, she does," Wales replied, understanding the coded reference.

They made their way to the commissary wagon on the camp's edge, where John Scobell, an average man to passersby, tended an open fire, stirring a large pot of stew for the troops. Though not an enlisted soldier, John held a trusted role as a civilian contractor, managing provisions and handling logistics—a position that allowed him to assist the regiment while remaining inconspicuous.

"John! A word if you will," Thomas greeted, shaking Scobell's hand. "How are things here?"

"Not bad," John replied, nodding. "Tonight's stew might be edible. A local farmer donated a cow, and we put it to effective use. A blessing, too, since we are running low on some essentials."

Thomas glanced at Wales, then back to John. "Aunt Todd might want to know about this," he said, using the code for their intelligence network. "Think we could arrange a letter home soon?"

John nodded, catching the implication. "Yes," he replied, his eyes glinting. "I think the old girl might need to hear a thing or two."

"The sooner, the better. But we must be cautious," Thomas added, his voice low.

"Wait," Wales interjected, his mind racing. "We need solid evidence before we make any accusations. Let us observe him, monitor his orders, and track any suspicious activities. If Church conspires against us, it falls to us to expose his duplicity."

Thomas and John nodded in agreement, a shared resolve forming among them. Wales steeled himself, knowing that if Church worked to undermine them, they would need to tread carefully, lest their own lives—and the fate of the regiment—be at risk.

*   *   *

How did I get here? Wales wondered, watching as Humphrey strode toward the new recruits drilling nearby. Nostalgically, he recalled the life he had left two years ago in New York. It seemed like forever since he had walked the quiet streets of Belvidere as well, his days absorbed in town planning and community building. Now, surrounded by the clamor of men preparing for war, he could not help but reflect on the strange path that had brought him to this place.

It had all started with a telegram—a simple message that had irrevocably altered the course of his life. On an otherwise ordinary day in his small storefront office on Main Street, the message arrived, bringing news that had shaken him to his core. Someone was coming, it had said, someone who would change everything.

Two years had passed, and the war with the southern states raged on. When he first signed up to help the Federals, his role was quiet, almost invisible. He would send occasional telegrams to update them on any suspected rebel activity in town and receive a modest payment in return. The town had stayed quiet; Wales saw no other agents and heard nothing back from the Federals—until now.

That mysterious "someone" turned out to be none other than Thomas Humphrey, a figure from Wales's past whose arrival signaled an unexpected new chapter in their shared history.

Thomas had filled him in on his life since their last meeting. Employed by the Pinkerton Detective Agency, Thomas worked for the Union Army, his assignments now tied to Major General George B. McClellan and the emerging Military Intelligence Service.

"I was stationed in Cincinnati under Major E.J. Allen," Thomas had explained, his eyes gleaming with a hint of pride. "The man swears by the motto, 'We never sleep!' and for good reason. When we escorted President Lincoln safely to Washington D.C. in time for his inauguration, I hardly slept a wink for days."

Then, in a quieter tone, Thomas had added, "Now President Lincoln himself has selected us for a critical mission. We are here to organize a regiment in Belvidere—a regiment of spies serving the Union cause."

Wales remembered the moment. His head had spun as Thomas laid out the plan. "I didn't agree with all of it," Thomas continued, his voice laced with irritation. "They assigned Colonel John Church to lead the 95th Illinois, a man who does not fully understand our purpose. I am Lieutenant Colonel of this 'merry band,' and you, my dear friend, are to serve as 2nd Lieutenant. Your task will be to handle the paperwork, coordinate dispatches, and"—Thomas's eyes gleamed with meaning— "help us communicate with a certain 'family member.' You understand, of course, that we will be writing to our dear 'Aunt Todd.'"

"Aunt Todd?" Wales had asked, a flicker of realization dawning on him. "You mean… Lincoln?"

"Well, yes, and his inner circle," Thomas confirmed. "The Todds, you see, are a big family. Lincoln's wife's given name," he added with a knowing smile.

At those words, Wales felt a wave of conflicting emotions. Duty tugged at him—he could hardly turn his back on his country in its hour of need. But there was also fear: fear of the unknown, fear of failure, fear of the dangerous road he was about to walk.

"Are you sure about this, Thomas?" he had asked, his voice barely steady. "I'm uncertain I'm cut out for this kind of work."

Thomas's gaze had hardened, his conviction unmistakable. "We all have a role to play, Wales. This is ours. We must do what is right, even if it is challenging."

With a knot of trepidation in his stomach, Wales had thrown himself into the task. Together with Thomas and a small but determined group, he had recruited men for the 95th Illinois Regiment. It was a challenge that assessed his limits, but as the regiment's ranks swelled with eager volunteers, he found himself caught up in a shared sense of purpose.

*   *   *

Amidst the clang of swords and the steady shuffle of boots on the training grounds, Wales observed the men of the 95th Illinois Regiment. Each day of rigorous practice and shared hardship transformed them from strangers into something like a family. Yet, even as he grew close to these men, the memory of Rebecca lingered, refusing to fade.

He had tried to move on, attempting to see other women when he first arrived in Belvidere, but none of them could hold his interest. Every conversation, every smile, reminded him of the way Rebecca had looked at him, her wit and fire leaving a mark he could not shake. *I wonder where you are now,* gazing at the surrounding men. *Probably married by now, settled into the life you were always meant for.*

Wales noticed John Scobell approaching. "A beautiful sight, isn't it?" John's voice was low, steady. "My father never would have imagined so many people fighting for his freedom. He died a slave, but his children and grandchildren will be free. This terrible institution will end."

Wales glanced at him, recognizing the deep, personal weight behind John's words. "You have my word, John," he replied with solemn resolve. "No man may own another. It is a sin in the eyes of God. This war will cost us dearly, but it must end here."

John nodded, his gaze steady. "I'm willing to pay that cost," he said. "I have spent my life knowing my family's suffering, knowing how many of us endured brutality in silence. My mother used to say freedom was a dream that no one in our family would live to see. I told her she would be wrong."

"Frederick Douglass says that without struggle, there can be no progress," John remarked, his eyes fixed on the soldiers' training in the field, his face set with quiet conviction.

Wales had no reply; he nodded in silent respect. He knew that John's role went far beyond that of a simple civilian contractor. Through their time together, Wales had learned that John worked for the Pinkerton Detective Agency, using his position as the commissary wagon manager to keep a close watch on camp activities, intercept messages, and quietly gather intelligence. To the men, John was just the man who managed supplies. But to those who knew, he was a critical part of the Union's intelligence network, quietly passing information that could alter the course of the war.

"Sometimes I wonder why I'm here, and then I remember the men like my father, like my grandfather, who had no choice," John continued, his voice a whisper. "I choose this fight, not just for myself, but for all of them. And for those who will come after. My children, and theirs. It must end with us."

Wales felt the weight of John's words. Here was a man generation of suffering forged whose resolve, and who lived his life by Douglass's words. *Without struggle, there can be no progress.* Wales felt a profound respect for John, a man who served a cause far beyond simple duty, a cause embedded in his very soul.

"John, you're more than you seem," Wales said softly, his voice filled with admiration.

John smiled, his eyes glinting. "Aren't we all?" He nodded, then turned back to the men drilling in the field, his expression one of quiet, unshakable resolve.

As Wales watched John slip back into his daily work, he felt a renewed sense of purpose. His respect for John and his mission grew, and he thought once more of Rebecca. She would always had a way of seeing things in him he hadn't seen himself, pushing him to be better, more courageous, even as they'd moved into New York's polished society circles. Here, surrounded by the rough edges of war, he wondered what she would think of him now.

Beneath the laughter and camaraderie of camp life, there was always solemnity, a reminder of the darkness awaiting them on the battlefield. And in the quiet of his tent at night, his memory returned to her again. The way she had looked at him, the spark in her eyes—he could not forget it. *Would she remember me?* He wondered. *Or have I become someone even I would not recognize?*

*   *   *

As flames flickered and shadows danced across their faces, Wales and Humphrey huddled close to the fire, locked in a hushed, intense conversation about the troubling behavior of Colonel Church. Humphrey's expression grew serious as he leaned in, his voice low, barely cutting through the crackle of the fire.

"I've noticed strange inconsistencies with Church," Humphrey muttered, his gaze hardening. "He has been disappearing at odd hours, claiming to be too sick to perform his duties, yet he slips out of his tent. And I have found him slashing supply orders for the regiment. Provisions spoiled, ammunition missing… this is not just incompetence—it's sabotage."

Wales nodded, the implications weighing heavily. "It's suspicious, but without solid evidence, we can't make a move."

Humphrey's jaw tightened. "Then maybe it's time to send word to Aunt Todd—if you catch my drift."

They knew that time was running out, especially with their orders to report to Louisville, Kentucky, for new duties under Major General H.G. Wright. The regiment could not afford a saboteur in their midst. Wales and Humphrey agreed to continue their surveillance, and as the days passed, they documented every questionable act.

One evening, they followed Colonel Church as he slipped away from camp under the cover of darkness. Moving stealthily, they shadowed him through the dense trees and brambles, careful to keep their distance while staying close enough to track his every move. The faint glow of his lantern bobbed ahead, casting fleeting glimpses of his face, tense and alert. Finally, Church stopped near a massive, hollowed-out tree on the camp's edge—a perfect location for a secret exchange.

Wales and Humphrey concealed themselves behind a thicket, holding their breath as they watched Church remove a small, paper-wrapped package from his coat. With a furtive glance around, he placed it inside the hollow trunk. He lingered for a moment, scanning the shadows as if sensing someone's eyes upon him, before turning and slipping back into the night.

They waited until they could no longer hear his footsteps before Humphrey nudged Wales. "Quick, man. Get it from the tree," he whispered.

Wales nodded, moving forward in a low crouch. Every sound—the crack of a twig, the rustle of leaves—seemed amplified in the night's stillness. His pulse hammered in his ears as he reached the hollow and felt around for the packet. Just as his fingers closed around the string binding it, he froze, hearing the faint crunch of footsteps behind him. He pulled it out and crouched low, the darkness hiding him.

A figure emerged from the shadows—a young boy, around ten years old, eyes wide with nerves as he approached the tree, glancing around as if he were being watched. He was so close, Wales held his breath, pressing himself tightly against the tree, praying the shadows would keep him concealed.

The boy reached for the hollow, fingers brushing over the empty space where the packet should have been. Confused, he peered around, his eyes darting suspiciously towards where Wales crouched, only feet away. For a tense moment, their eyes nearly met, and Wales prepared to bolt, his heart pounding like a drum. But after a second, the boy backed away, his face pale with anxiety as he disappeared into the night.

Wales let out a slow, relieved breath, holding up the packet to show Humphrey before they slipped back into the cover of the trees.

"That's the proof we needed," Humphrey whispered, his voice barely audible. His face set with grim satisfaction as he took the packet from Wales and examined it in the moonlight.

"Look at this! It is a note informing the Confederates we are heading into Mississippi soon!" said exclaimed Thomas. "Now, let's get back before anyone else comes snooping around."

Back at camp, Humphrey sent Wales to check if Church had returned to his tent. Slipping up to the tent flap, Wales peeked in and saw it was empty. He signaled to Humphrey, who returned with a small bottle. In the dim firelight, Wales could make out the label, but a grim instinct told him it was not medicinal. Humphrey entered Church's tent briefly, reemerging with a satisfied look.

"If he wasn't sick before, he soon will be," Humphrey murmured, a dark resolve in his voice. "Since our colonel has a fondness for drink, it is the perfect place to 'supplement' his evening routine."

The following day, Church returned, worse for wear, and soon polished off the drink in his tent. By nightfall, he was "too sick to perform duties," and Humphrey took charge, calling for the doctor. The next day, with Church bedridden, Humphrey became Acting Colonel of the 95th Illinois.

Standing before his assembled troops, Humphrey addressed them with calm authority. "Men, Colonel Church's health has taken a turn, we sent him home to recover. I will be taking on additional duties to ensure our mission proceeds without disruption."

A murmur of surprise rippled through the ranks, but when Drillmaster Sellers asked who would lead them, Humphrey reassured them, "I will. We will remain focused and united. We have a job to do, and nothing will stop us from fulfilling it."

As the troops dispersed, Wales and Humphrey stayed by the fire, sharing a rare moment of quiet.

"We did what was necessary," Wales said, his gaze fixed on the flames.

Humphrey nodded. "And we will keep doing what's right. For the men, and for the mission—no matter what it takes."

Chapter Five

Since arriving at Camp Fuller on September 3rd disguised as Albert Cashin, Rebecca kept her voice low, her cap pulled down to shade her face, obscuring any hint of her identity. She noticed that even the youngest recruits smeared dirt on their upper lips, a feeble attempt at appearing older, marked by a shadow of a mustache.

Oh, the things I must do to remain hidden! How can I approach you with no one knowing the truth? Rebecca's eyes misted as she glanced toward the officers' tents where Wales worked. She spotted his familiar figure moving about, his bright blond hair unmistakable in the sunlight. Seeing him now, mature, and formidable in his Union uniform, tightened something in her chest.

At first, Rebecca was anxious about being discovered, but the size of the 95th Regiment provided her with ample cover. Among over nine hundred men, blending in felt manageable, a sea of bodies and chaos. Better yet, when the Seventy-fourth, Ninety-Second, and Ninety-Sixth Illinois Infantry joined them at Camp Fuller, the sheer numbers allowed her to slip further into anonymity.

Clenching her jaw, she whispered, *you can do this*. She willed her voice to hold steady against the surge of nerves in her chest. She stayed close to the younger recruits, those who seemed as green as she was, creating the perfect cover for a woman trying to pass as a young man.

But life in the regiment turned out to be far harder than she had expected. She had assumed the older soldiers would ease up on the newer recruits, give them time to adjust to the demands of camp life. But she had been wrong. The veterans pushed them, barking orders, demanding strength from the young recruits, assessing their limits without mercy. It was far from the camaraderie or guidance she had expected. Each day, she faced not just physical challenges but also the struggle to keep up the act, to remain unseen as Rebecca within the role of Albert.

Despite the grueling work, the aching muscles, and the constant anxiety, she felt something else—an exhilaration she had not expected. The intensity of each drill, each maneuver, brought a surge of adrenaline she found addictive. She was training like the men she had grown up watching, taking on the same grueling routines, feeling herself grow stronger, harder. The physical pain was something she could manage; the mental sharpness required was a thrilling game of survival.

"Hey, Bert!" A loud slap landed on her back, and she turned to see Samuel Peppers grinning at her. "Knew I would find ya. We are bunking together, sharing a tent. The boys who have seen battle are roughing it with wood shelters. But us greenhorns get tents out back. Guess they are prepping us for the field."

"Oh, sure," she replied, the reality of sharing a tent hitting her like a shock of freezing water. Any hope for her own space evaporated. She had seen how Samuel treated women back in town. Rowdy, but at least decent.

I can just imagine the ladies in New York gossiping about this. She tried not to blush. She had never seen her father without a shirt, and now here she was, living with a man.

Samuel looked her over, smirking. "City boy, huh? You got that soft look about ya."

Rebecca nodded, forcing a smile. "Yeah, you could say that," keeping her voice steady despite her anxiety.

"Figured." Samuel's face softened with a grin. "Stick with me, then. We are green too. You will get the hang of it."

Rebecca offered a nod, relieved her disguise seemed to hold. They moved through the bustling camp, weaving around piles of lumber and scattered tools. The sounds of hammers and saws filled the air, mixed with barked orders and occasional laughter from more seasoned soldiers.

They reached their assigned tent, a modest setup with just enough room for two cots and their gear. She claimed a bed farthest from the entrance, taking a deep breath as she arranged her belongings, feeling the weight of her hidden wardrobe—a skirt, blouse, the handkerchief Wales gave her, and a light hat—tucked into the bottom of her pack.

You never know, she reflected. If *they find out, I might need to change and slip away.* Samuel distracted her, "So, what did ya do before all this? Why would you sign up?"

Rebecca shrugged, her mind racing to weave a believable backstory. "Worked in a kitchen, baking mostly. Wanted to do something more meaningful." Her voice was steady, but her insides knotted with nerves.

Samuel nodded with understanding. "Farmhand here. Challenging work, but nothin' like this."

Rebecca smiled faintly. "We will get the hang of it. Just takes time."

Suddenly, a stern voice echoed outside. "Recruits! Fall in for roll call!"

Rebecca's heart leapt. She exchanged a quick glance with Samuel before they hurried outside, to the line of new recruits gathering in the clearing. She stood rigid, eyes fixed forward, hoping her disguise would withstand close inspection.

An officer walked down the line, his gaze sharp and scrutinizing. He stopped in front of Rebecca, eyeing her with a hint of suspicion.

"Name?" he barked.

"Albert Cashin," she replied.

The officer raised a brow. "Son, you do not look a day over fourteen. Could have waited until you shaved to sign up." He shook his head and moved on, leaving Rebecca to exhale sharply.

"Alright, listen up!" the officer addressed the group. "We have work to do and not time. You are green, but you will learn. Stick together, follow orders, and we will make soldiers out of you. We are waiting on supplies, and uniforms will be issued once they arrive."

The recruits dispersed, and Rebecca felt a flicker of hope. She could pull this off after all. Samuel clapped her on the shoulder, grinning.

"Come on, Bert," he said. "Let us show 'em what we can do."

Each day started before dawn with grueling squad drills. Rebecca's legs burned as she ran obstacle courses, her breath measured and steady. For Samuel, mornings seemed simple—shirt, trousers, and he was ready. But Rebecca had a ritual, sneaking off to "shit and shave" by the creek to wrap her chest with a strip of cotton cloth she had swiped from the surgeon's supplies.

Thank God I am small-chested, she was grateful not to have her sister's fuller figure.

The drills were unrelenting, designed to break them down and rebuild them as soldiers. She adapted to the weight of her pack, once unbearable, now almost familiar. Even the physical toll affected her differently; the intensity shortened her monthly cycle to a minor inconvenience, manageable with a thick rag.

Training was chaotic when it came to learning the regiment's complex drill routines. Officers struggled with the intricate commands, their inexperience painfully clear, and the troops stumbled over each other as they tried to follow. Rebecca felt awkward at first, her limbs tangling with each maneuver, but repetition soon turned the disarray into something resembling rhythm. She learned to pivot and sidestep coordinated with the others, becoming one with the regiment's pulse.

Evenings brought respite, with brief meals and lectures on tactics and strategy. Exhaustion weighed her down, but Rebecca fought to stay alert, absorbing every detail. She was determined to prove herself, sharpening her mind with each session.

They do not teach this at finishing school, she thought wryly, learning about sword parts as if it were embroidery.

Samuel often struggled beside her, grumbling as he stumbled through drills. "Feels like I got two left feet, Bert!" He groaned one morning.

Rebecca managed a faint smile, hiding her relief that she had learned the sequences without missing a beat. She was changing—her hands, once soft, now calloused, her shoulders stronger, her stride more confident.

One evening, as she finished work near the supply tent, she turned a corner and nearly collided with Wales who was stepping out from the officers' area his eyes briefly widening in surprise. For a heartbeat, they stood face-to-face, closer than they had been since she arrived.

"Watch it, Private," he muttered gruffy. Yet his eyes lingered, studying her face with a glimmer of something—recognition, or just curiosity.

Does he recognize me? The question hammered in her mind, and her breath caught, but she forced herself to look down, pulling her cap a little lower. "Apologies, sir," she murmured, her voice steady, though her pulse raced.

Wales frowned, his gaze tracing her features with a hint of familiarity. "You… remind me of someone," he murmured, to himself.

Rebecca's heart twisted. She wanted so badly to reach out, to whisper something only he would understand, but a sharp voice interrupted them from nearby.

"Lieutenant Wood! The captain's waiting on your report!"

Wales straightened at once, his face hardening. The brief, almost tender look was gone, replaced by the rigid mask of duty. With one last, lingering glance, he nodded to her, then turned and strode away toward the officer's tent.

Rebecca stood there, rooted in place, watching him until he disappeared, her heart aching with words she could not say. She had been so close, yet circumstances had stolen the moment from her. It was for the best. Timing was everything, and tonight, it was not right.

With a soft sigh, she turned and melted back into the camp's shadows, her resolve hardening once more.

*   *   *

Since arriving at Camp Fuller on September 3rd, Rebecca, disguised as Albert Cashin, had become determined to stay hidden in plain sight. The relentless drills and duties took a toll on her body, and though she grew stronger each day, she could not keep up with the others in every way. As a woman her strength would never match theirs, and neither would her height. While the younger boys would grow, she was as tall as she would ever be.

She needed something more to keep up her ruse—something that could make her indispensable. That is when she remembered her unique skill: the art of transforming basic ingredients into a meal worth savoring. If she could make their meager rations taste better, the men would value her presence. Observing the food supplies, she cataloged each item mentally. Then she tracked the information down in her notebook. Rebecca focused on plotting ways to make simple meals enjoyable.

One evening by the fire, she jotted down ideas in her notebook, noting the ingredients they received and the small possibilities for improving them. A smile tugged at her lips as she envisioned ways to spice up the bland diet. She could almost hear her mother's voice: *The way to a man's heart is through his stomach.* Well, maybe it was also the way to a soldier's respect.

That night, as she sat by the fire, she overheard Private Thornhill dictated a letter to his wife. Not all the soldiers knew how to write, so his bunkmate wrote down his words. His tone was lighthearted, his voice carrying in the cool night air. "I have to admit, we're getting along pretty well here so far," he chuckled. "We've got plenty to eat—cornmeal, flour, sugar, coffee, molasses, peas, pork… and they say we'll get beef soon, though I've yet to see it." His eyes twinkled as he cast a sidelong glance at his companions. "Some of you boys could use that vinegar and soap as soon as it gets here. It will help with the smell. I will say that much!"

Rebecca stifled a laugh, feeling a sense of camaraderie around the fire. Thornhill's humor helped lift the mood, and she realized familiar food flavors might do the same. Tucking her notebook back into her pack, she resolved to experiment, hoping her cooking could become her contribution to the group.

In the days that followed, Rebecca's knack for turning rations into something flavorful gained her a reputation in camp. Each improvement—a dash of salt in the coffee, a tender bit of salted pork stewed with peas—felt like a small offering, a quiet bond with the surrounding men. Soldiers began gathering by her fire, savoring the simple warmth of good flavor amidst the rough camp life. Her cooking was not just about feeding them; it was a way of lifting their spirits, keeping them going with a taste of home.

One evening, as she was tending a small pot over the fire, George Bennette, a man from Company B, appeared silently by her side and placed a larger tin coffee pot over the flames. He poured her small coffee pot's contents into the larger one, adding enough ground beans to make a stronger brew for the whole group. "I'll fetch more firewood," he murmured before disappearing into the woods, leaving her and Samuel in stunned silence.

Samuel chuckled, clapping her shoulder. "George is a quiet man, but when he does talk, you'd best listen," he said with a grin. "We have all seen what you are doing here. You keep turning scraps into something worth eating, and we will manage the rest."

Samuel leaned in, lowering his voice. "I spotted a poor, lonely chicken over the hill earlier. Do not know how it escaped, but we will get it. Think you can whip it into something decent?"

Rebecca grinned, lowering her voice to maintain her disguise. "Sure," she replied, her heart swelled at the camaraderie forming around her. She realized she needed this bond with the men as much as they needed her cooking.

When the supply wagons arrived at camp on September 26th, the recruits received their full kits— canteens, haversacks, and much-needed undergarments. The issuing of equipment signaled their imminent departure, and Rebecca felt an urgency to speak with Wales in private. She watched him from afar as he climbed the supply wagons, organizing bundles and directing the distribution.

As the recruits lined up to collect their gear, Rebecca fell into place, watching as the line inched forward. She felt her pulse quicken as she drew closer to Wales, seeing him within arm's reach, working with an intensity that commanded attention. He seemed lost in his task, but then, just as she approached the front, his gaze lifted and found her. For a moment, his eyes lingered on her, a flicker of curiosity or recognition flashing in their depths.

Her breath caught, and she looked away, her heart hammering as she kept her face hidden under her cap, hoping he would not look too closely. But she felt his gaze remain on her seconds longer, as though something about her seemed familiar, tugging at the edge of his memory. She dared a quick glance back, meeting his eyes just briefly before he turned away, returning to his work.

When she reached the front of the line, she accepted her pack from the quartermaster, aware of Wales standing just behind him, shifting bundles, and calling out instructions. She was so close she could hear the steady cadence of his voice, calm yet firm, guiding the men with the ease of a seasoned leader.

Rebecca's heart twisted with a pang of regret, knowing she could not reveal herself. She had come within feet of him, but with so many men around, there was no way to say what was on her mind. She clenched her jaw and held her kit close, forcing herself to keep moving down the line. This fleeting moment, though charged with unspoken words, would have to be enough—for now.

As the recruits filed away from the supply wagon, a physician arrived to conduct a final health check, his presence sparking new anxiety in Rebecca. Standing in line with the others, she fought to keep her expression neutral, though her heart raced at enduring a physical examination. How thorough would it be? How close might he look?

"Next!" called out the physician, a portly man with an unyielding gaze motioned her forward.

With a steadying breath, Rebecca stepped up, her fingers gripping the edge of her cap as she kept her head down, hoping to shield her face. The doctor's eyes narrowed as he looked her over, taking in her slender frame with an expression that comforted her.

"What's your age, son?" he asked, his tone more probing than friendly.

"Eighteen, sir," she replied, deepening her voice and hoping her answer would satisfy him.

The physician raised an eyebrow. "Eighteen, you say. Small for eighteen." He leaned closer, his eyes sharp and assessing as they traveled over her frame. "I see some of these young ones tryin' to join early, barely fifteen or sixteen," he added, his gaze fixed on her as though trying to peel back her disguise. "Haven't hit your growth spurt yet, have you?"

Rebecca's stomach twisted. She forced a shrug. "Not yet, sir. But I am strong, and I can do the work." She attempted to project confidence despite the knots tightening in her gut.

The doctor tilted his head, his eyes not leaving her face. "Strong, are you?" He extended his hand. "Show me your grip."

Rebecca's heart raced as she took his hand, pressing down with all the strength she could muster. The physician's eyebrows rose as he felt her effort, though she sensed that her grip was weaker than he expected. He pursed his lips, his gaze traveling back to her slender shoulders, a skeptical glint in his eye.

"Let's see you lift that pack over there." He pointed to a bulky bag filled with extra gear.

Rebecca swallowed hard, forcing herself to remain calm. She strode to the pack and lifted it, feeling her muscles strain as she hoisted it over her shoulder. She gritted her teeth, fighting to appear at ease under the doctor's watchful eyes. When she set it down, she felt the weight of his scrutiny pressing on her more than on the pack itself.

The physician frowned, not fully convinced, and stepped closer; his gaze now focused on her face. "Why don't you look at me straight on, son?"

Rebecca's pulse raced, but she lifted her head, meeting his gaze and attempting a steady expression. The doctor's sharp eyes studied her features, and for a tense moment, she felt as if he could see right through her disguise. Her heart pounded as she forced herself to stand still, praying he would move on.

After a long, uncomfortable silence, the doctor leaned back, as though weighing his options. He gave a curt nod. "Two good eyes, two good hands, and two good feet," he declared, though there was a trace of suspicion in his tone. "Fit for service." He glanced down at his clipboard, making a note before moving on to the next recruit.

Rebecca released a shaky breath, barely able to contain her relief. She turned away, feeling the tension leave her body in waves, but the relief was fleeting. She knew she had barely passed, that the doctor's eyes would be on her again if she wasn't careful. Yet she had made it—she was officially in.

With her heart still pounding, she stepped forward to take the oath, her voice strong as she repeated the words that would seal her place in the regiment.

"I, Albert Cashin, do solemnly swear that I will bear true allegiance to the United States of America and serve them honestly and faithfully against all their enemies or opposers whatsoever; and observe and obey the orders of the officers appointed over me, according to the Rules and Articles for the government of the armies of the United States."

As she finished, Rebecca felt a strange mix of pride and apprehension settle in her chest. She had passed the first real hurdle of this dangerous game, and there was no turning back now.

After the oath, she made her way to the supply wagon, where she received her new uniform and supplies. With careful hands, she accepted her kit, the weight of it solidifying her role. Soon, she would march alongside these men, facing the unknown challenges together.

*   *   *

Weeks had passed since she left New York and Belvidere. Weeks of travel, drilling, and trying to find the right moment to talk to Wales. But he was a lieutenant, and she was a private. Wales was an adjunct for the entire regiment and was leaving or returning to the camp and was never alone.

I can either lean into whatever this is or stick around. Rebecca decided. Waiting for the right moment seemed like the current call to action.

Rebecca, as Albert, immersed herself in the demanding routine of training. She learned to march with precision, every step synchronized with her comrades. The discipline of the drill instilled in her a sense of unity and purpose, forging bonds that transcended individuality.

From dawn until dusk, Rebecca drilled, the rhythmic cadence of marching echoing through the camp. "Left! Left! Left! Right, Left!" The commands resounded, guiding the soldiers in perfect unison.

For Rebecca, the food became her armor as much as her disguise. As she watched Wales work by the supply wagons, she thought it would also be her way of bridging the gap between them, one cup of spiced coffee at a time.

One evening, Rebecca tried recreating a dessert she had heard about called "hard tack apple pie." She took the rock-hard crackers and broke them into a pot, covering them with water to soften. Once softened, she mixed in raisins, spices and chopped apples, forming the mixture into small cakes.

As the pie baked over the fire, the sweet aroma wafted through the camp. Soon, curious soldiers gathered round, marveling at the treat Rebecca had conjured from their meager supplies.

When they bit into the pie, the men's eyes lit up. "Reminds me of my auntie's apple pie back home!" one exclaimed. Rebecca smiled, warmed to see them savor this small pleasure amid hardship.

After that, the men awaited to see what she whipped up next with their limited ingredients. Her skills not only nourished their bodies, but their spirits, too.

As the 95th Regiment divided into ten companies, Rebecca and Samuel found themselves assigned to Company G under the leadership of Captain Elliot Bush. There they learned the exciting part of the training; the proper techniques for loading and firing a weapon. Rebecca had to admit this was her favorite part. The anticipation of the blast of the gun followed by the fall of the wooden target thrilled her unlike anything else.

This is certainly something I can get used to, as she loaded another shot and fired the musket again. The practice of using the gun while they marched, lined up, and various movements on the battlefield was also electrifying.

Marching orders soon followed. On the 29th day at Camp Fuller, they ordered the 95th Illinois to entrain for Louisville, Kentucky. There they would bolster the forces of Major General Henry W. Wright, Commander of the Department of the Ohio.

*　　*　　*

Fear gnawed at Rebecca's heart. The farther south they traveled, the closer they drew to battle. While her comrades were eager for their first taste of combat, she felt trepidation. She remembered the reports from the newspapers back home in New York, stories of brave young men who never made it home.

As the regiment pushed forward, Samuel, her bunkmate and closest friend, noticed her silence and mistook it for disappointment at not having seen a fight yet. With a sympathetic smile, he joined her.

"Timing is everything in this game," Samuel's voice warm and reassuring. "We'll get our chance soon enough."

Rebecca forced a half-smile, looking up at him. "Better later than sooner, Samuel. Much later."

Their march brought them to Abbeville, Mississippi, where they camped until December 18th. News soon arrived that Confederate General Van Dorn had raided Holly Springs, surprising the Federal garrison and destroying a critical supply depot for General Grant's army. Holly Springs had been a vital source of provisions, so its loss was a devastating blow.

With little time to absorb the news, General Van Dorn ordered the 95th Regiment to pursue Van Dorn, only to find that he had slipped away again. The march was grueling, more exhausting than anything Rebecca had endured, leaving her legs feeling as though they had been carved from stone.

"Van Dorn's got a knack for slipping away," one soldier grumbled as they made their way back to camp, worn from the futile chase. Word soon came that Van Dorn had retreated to Grenada, and any hope of an encounter was gone.

Rebecca forced a frustrated expression, but inside, she felt an unexpected sense of relief to not fight. The intensity of the march alone was enough to remind her of what lay ahead, and she knew a full battle would test them in ways they could scarcely imagine.

"We'll catch him eventually," she said, masking her relief with a tone of forced resolve.

Under the constant strain of their march, Rebecca's body transformed. Muscles she hadn't known existed were now defined and strong. Her endurance had increased tenfold, and she found herself able to carry her gear for miles without faltering. The early days of soreness and fatigue had given way to resilience; her steps were now steady, her pace unwavering.

One evening, as they set up camp, Samuel glanced over at her with a playful grin. "You know, Bert, you're not the same green recruit who couldn't tell a rifle from a shovel."

Rebecca laughed, surprised at how good it felt to share in the camaraderie. "Guess we're all changing, aren't we?"

Samuel's grin faded, his expression growing serious. "Yeah. War does that. But we have got each other's backs, and that makes all the difference."

Chapter Six

"Sir, thank you for your time," said Captain Elliott Bush of the 95th Illinois Company G. to Thomas, "We're dealing with a rather unusual situation."

The regiment traveled south, sometimes by train or steamer, other times on foot, fighting against the winter chill that crept into their tents. It was January 18, 1863, and they had passed through Memphis, Tennessee, setting up camp three days after in rural Mississippi. They had just received news that Pemberton, following the disaster at Holly Springs, had retreated into Louisiana.

"Certainly, Captain Bush, how can we assist?" asked Corporal Thomas Humphrey, as Wales readied his quill and ink, laying out paper on his travel desk in their officer's tent.

Bush cleared his throat. "It is about Private Cashin. The men have taken quite a liking to his cooking—so much so that it is causing problems. They leave their posts, making excuses to linger near his campfire. It has become a bit of a… disruption."

Corporal Humphrey raised an eyebrow, leaning back. "A good cook can lift spirits, no doubt, but too much of a good thing can lead to trouble. What do you suggest, Captain?"

Bush glanced at Wales, who was jotting down notes with swift, practiced strokes. "We need to manage the demand. We cannot have half the company neglecting their duties just to get a taste of Cashin's cooking."

Wales paused, his quill hovering over the paper. He felt an inexplicable pull toward Albert from the start, a kind of quiet fascination that left him uneasy. He watched the way Albert moved, the quiet confidence and poise that seemed out of place for a soldier. He tried to reason it away—it was just the isolation of camp life, the lack of female companionship stirring emotions he had never had reason to question. But the feeling lingered, unsettling, and foreign.

He had dismissed it as a mere curiosity at first, something born of the long nights and cold winds. Yet, as he observed Albert, he could not shake the feeling. He was not one to be drawn to men, but this felt different, confusingly familiar, and it gnawed at him. The subtle grace, the quiet gestures—it reminded him of something, someone from a life he had left behind.

"Perhaps we could meet with Cashin and discuss the situation," Wales suggested, pushing away his confusion to focus on the matter at hand. "Maybe even transfer him to collaborate with John Scobell in the supply wagon. It could spread the responsibility—and the popularity. With spirits so low after Holly Springs, it may help morale in a controlled way."

"Scobell's dependable," Humphrey agreed. "Having Cashin with him could maintain the quality of the meals while ensuring discipline. Besides, Scobell's duties require someone with a steady hand and a sharp eye."

"Agreed," Bush nodded. "Let us speak with Cashin, and we might involve his bunkmate, Samuel Peppers, too. He has got a knack for drawing people in and already helps Cashin with the food."

As they made their way across camp, passing rows of tents and soldiers huddled around fires, Wales felt a familiar tug again, a strange unease that he could not shake. The name Cashin stirred something in him, something beyond the present. It was not common, and he was almost certain Rebecca had no brother. Could there be some other connection?

He frowned, pushing the thought aside as the scent of something unexpected hit him—apple pie? He wondered where they had got apples.

They found Cashin busy at the fire, lifting the lid on a pan as soldiers chatted nearby, looking forward to the meal. Another whiff of apple reached Wales' nose.

Cashin's back was to them, but as he straightened and turned, wiping his hands on an apron, Samuel Peppers stood and saluted. "Hey, Albert! Looks like we have visitors."

Cashin turned to greet the officers. "Captain, Corporal…Lieutenant…" he said, with a polite nod, his voice steady.

Wales studied Cashin's face, feeling a chill as his suspicions crystallized. The softness in Cashin's features, the way he moved with subtle grace—he realized with sudden clarity. A memory triggered from years before, of the woman he had left behind in New York.

Rebecca Cashin.

He froze, his quill slipping from his hand. *It is her,* his heart pounded. All the strange feelings, the inexplicable attraction—they suddenly made sense. It was not Albert he had been drawn to all along. It was

Rebecca, disguised and hidden, but still unmistakably the woman he had left behind.

Unaware of Wales' realization, Humphrey continued, "Cashin, we have been discussing a new arrangement. Your cooking has become popular, and it is creating a bit of disorder. We want to move you and Private Peppers to collaborate with John Scobell in the supply wagon. How does that sound?"

Rebecca—Cashin—nodded. "I am happy to serve wherever I am needed, Corporal. If working with Scobell helps, I am at your disposal."

"Whoo-hoo!" Samuel exclaimed, slapping his thigh. "Albert, you got us the best spot in camp with those good vittles!"

Wales felt his heart pounding but kept his face neutral. He knew it was her, but now was not the time for revelations. Too many eyes, too many ears. "Very good, then. We will arrange the transfer," His voice sounded steadier than he felt.

As they turned to leave, Wales bent to pick up his fallen quill, casting one last look back. Rebecca—or rather, Albert—was already busy again, the familiar figure now cloaked in mystery. He knew he would confront her soon, but for now, he'd keep his discovery to himself.

*   *   *

Thoughts of Rebecca—and the daring choices that had brought her to the 95th—haunted Wales as he watched her move through camp. He had often seen her working alongside Samuel in John Scobell's supply team, yet every chance to speak with her had slipped away.

Over time, Wales began catching trivial things that might have gone unnoticed had he not known her secret. While gambling, drinking, and profanity were all common pastimes in camp, Rebecca avoided them, maintaining a quiet discipline that set her apart. It mirrored his own restraint, though for him, it was more from habit than necessity.

He also realized something else: they both remained isolated in their own way. Just like him, she did not receive letters from home, nor did she send any. If anything happened to her, no family would receive word or come to claim her; she was entirely alone in this.

Word had arrived from "Auntie Todd" that President Lincoln had signed the Emancipation Proclamation on September 22nd, though it would not take effect until January 1st, 1863. For John—a freeman back in Illinois, now standing as a freeman in his birthplace of Mississippi—the news should have been a cause for celebration. Yet, when Wales delivered the news, John's reaction caught him off guard.

"Thank you, Wales," John said, nodding. "But it is one thing to see it written, another to see it happen. I will feel it in my heart when that day comes, but not before." Then, with a wry smile, he added, "Oh, and thanks for sending those two over from Company G. Albert's got away with grub that makes it almost tolerable, and Samuel's a diligent worker. You know Albert is… special, don't you? Took me a minute. She is good at hiding."

So, John Scobell, too, had noticed that there was something different about Albert.

John continued, "The young soldier was like any other—quiet, diligent, always willing to pull his weight—but his fastidiousness with hygiene is why I noticed. Whenever we worked with provisions or loaded supplies, Albert always stayed a little cleaner. Unlike the men, who carried the dust and sweat of the day, he keeps himself put-together."

"At first," said John, "I could not put his finger on it. But after watching Albert with growing curiosity, the truth struck me one day as he saw him— no, her—wiping her face and neck with a damp cloth after a long day of hauling crates. My instincts were right: Albert is a woman. You know, I later dropped a subtle hint to Samuel, thinking he might have noticed something, too. Samuel shrugged, giving me a confused look."

"Albert's a diligent worker," Samuel said. "Seems clean-cut, but we've all got our quirks."

"I hid my surprise, but then realized that Samuel had not even considered the possibility. After all, Samuel said he spent his life working on a farm with other men and had no reason to know the finer points of women's ways," he concluded.

Wales struggled to meet John's knowing gaze. "Umm… well."

John chuckled. "Alright, I hear you," he said. "But you'd better sort it out soon."

Wales retreated, his mind flustered, his heart racing.

*　　*　　*

With Grant calling for reinforcements to join the Army of the Tennessee, the 95th continued its relentless push south. On January 19th, they boarded the aging steamer *Maria Denning*, packed shoulder-to-shoulder with soldiers from the 11th Iowa Infantry, the 18th Wisconsin, and a company of the 2nd Illinois Artillery.

Below deck, horses, mules, army wagons, and artillery crowded every inch, adding to the oppressive atmosphere. Men sprawled across every available nook, grateful for any space they could claim.

Wales learned that Rebecca and Samuel had volunteered to remain below, assisting John Scobell in monitoring supplies, a task that kept them shuffling provisions in the cramped, swaying quarters. While most soldiers sought fresh air on the upper decks, Rebecca worked below, hidden from the others.

On January 26th, the fleet reached Milliken's Bend, and the men eagerly disembarked, leaving the close quarters of the ship behind. Soon after, the 95th received orders to march to Young's Point, Louisiana, where they worked at the grueling task of digging a canal intended to bypass Vicksburg's formidable defenses.

The work was relentless, day and night, and the surrounding land made it harder. The dense forest of tall cypress and live oak, their boughs draped in long drapes of Spanish moss, shut out every breeze.

The hot sun shone down through the stagnant air. Though it was called ground, there was no perceptible elevation; the lowlands of Louisiana were devoid of any pebble or stone, each particle of earth made from rotting trees and bushes.

As days stretched into weeks, they moved north to Lake Providence, where engineers aimed to breach the levee and flood the oxbow lake, hoping to create a potential route to the Red River.

The brutal digging, though exhausting, carried renewed energy when Adjutant General Lorenzo Thomas arrived from Washington, bearing orders to enlist formerly enslaved into the Union Army. With Black and white soldiers now working side-by-side, the camp buzzed with a new dynamic, a sense of history shifting beneath their feet, even in this sunbaked, mosquito-infested land.

Once the camp settled into a routine, Wales summoned Rebecca—still disguised as Private Cashin—to his tent. She entered, her apprehension barely concealed, eyes flicking around the room before settling on him. With Humphrey and General Thomas away, Wales motioned for her to keep her voice low.

"Albert," he began, his tone sharp, almost accusing. "I trust your assignment to the supply wagon is going well." This was the moment he had planned to confront her, to demand that she abandon this reckless charade and go home. But as he looked at her in her worn blue uniform, her face set with defiance and determination, words failed him.

Here she was, right in front of him, alive and real—so close he could reach out and touch her, confirm she was more than the feverish worry that had haunted him since the moment he knew she was here. Yet all he felt was anger, raw and smoldering beneath the surface.

"Sir? Wales, I have been waiting for this moment, I…" Her voice wavering, betraying the emotions she kept locked behind her disguise.

"Private Cashin," he interrupted, forcing formality, his words coming out sharper than he intended, "We are using the supply wagon to haul debris from the canal. Can you manage that along with your duties and provisions? Scobell says you have been a tremendous help." He was deflecting, stumbling, unable to articulate the surge of emotions roiling inside him.

Rebecca's brow furrowed. "Wales— Lieutenant Wood—you know who I am."

Wales' expression hardened as his anger took control. "I do not know what game you're playing, but we're on the edge of battle, and you can't fool me. I left you in New York. Why are you here?" The words tore out of him, heavy with frustration. "Do you realize what could happen if you are caught? If anyone discovered your identity, you could be jailed—or worse. And what would your family think if they found out?"

"They won't find out," she replied, a challenge in her voice. "But what about you? Do you think I came all this way to be scolded? I wanted to see you, Wales."

The confession tore something loose inside Wales. Rage flared, bright and consuming. She had risked everything—her life, her freedom—just to be near him, and all he wanted to do was reach out, pull her close, and hold her, touch her face, tell her how reckless and foolish and brave she was. But he could not give in to that impulse, not now.

He took a steady breath, fighting to keep his voice under control. "You came here to see me?" His words, laced with both disbelief and something softer, something he struggled to keep hidden. "Do you understand the consequences if you are discovered? They would accuse the regiment of fraud. Stripped of my commission. I would face court-martial."

Her gaze softened, though her resolve remained unbroken. "Then maybe you should understand why I am here. Do you think I put myself through this without a reason?"

Her words twisted the knife deeper, igniting his anger again. He wanted to shake her, to make her see the impossible danger she was courting just by standing here. "I want to send you home, but you can't leave now," His voice dropped to a low, intense murmur, every word heavy with unspent fury and contained fear. "We are in rebel territory. Do you understand what could happen if they find out? The men might not see you as…well, as a soldier."

Tears pricked her eyes, but she blinked them away, lifting her chin in defiance. The sight fueled his frustration, stirring feelings he was not ready to confront.

Seeing her pain, a crack formed in his anger, allowing his own emotions to seep through. "We are both risking everything, Rebecca. But if you are found out, it is a matter of time before they act against you— or worse. Keep it secret and I will figure something out."

She dropped her gaze, gathering herself, and after a long moment, nodded. "Alright. I hate this damn war."

Wales felt a wave of relief wash over him, tempered by the lingering ache of anger and helplessness. He wanted to reach for her, to do something that would break through the anger and fear. But he clenched his fists instead, forcing himself to stay rooted where he was. "Thank you."

As she turned to leave, he watched her go, leaving him with his emotions churning, a tangled knot of anger, fear, and longing.

*   *   *

The next evening, as the men huddled around their fires for warmth, he watched her and John struggling to free the supply wagon from a deep rut in the mud. Corporal Thomas Humphrey stood nearby, observing, his gaze fixed on their efforts.

Rebecca sat on the buckboard, guiding the horses, while John labored at the wheel, trying to gain traction in the stubborn, soaked soil. As Rebecca urged the lead horse forward, the wagon lurched, and a heavy crate of supplies slid toward the edge. Wales's heart jumped as Rebecca caught the crate with one hand and pulled the horses back with the other, halting the wagon and steadying the precarious load.

Relief washed over him—until he noticed something that made his stomach clench. The effort had loosened her jacket just enough to reveal the bindings she used to conceal her true figure. In that instant, Wales saw Corporal Humphrey's eyebrows raise as realization dawned on his face. Rebecca, quick to react, clutched her jacket closed, but the brief slip had already done its damage.

Wales moved quickly, reaching Thomas before he could say a word. The flickering firelight cast long shadows over the camp as Wales drew close. "Thomas, we need to talk," he muttered, his voice low and tense.

Thomas looked at him with raised eyebrows, a glint of amusement in his eyes. "Do we now? What clandestine secrets has my lieutenant been hiding?"

"Albert…Rebecca…is a surprise to us both," Wales looked away.

Thomas's smirk widened. "Rebecca? Well, he—or rather, she—is indeed full of surprises."

Wales glanced back at Rebecca, still flustered as she steadied the wagon. She caught his eye, and in the brief exchange, he saw panic flash across her face before she looked away.

As the wagon broke free, John joined her on the buckboard, wiping his hands on his trousers. Wales fell silent, his mind whirling with the conflict.

The revelation of her identity had shaken him, and now Thomas knew. How was he supposed to keep her safe now?

Thomas studied him, a mixture of curiosity and amusement on his face. "She has been here, doing everything a soldier does. Who is she, to hide so well among us? And why is she here?"

Wales swallowed, choosing his words carefully. "I met her in New York. We were…acquaintances. Crossed paths a few times—nothing more."

Thomas's gaze sharpened. "And you did not suspect anything when she turned up here, in your regiment? Doesn't that strike you as strange?"

Wales shook his head, feeling the strain of keeping his anger and worry in check. "Not until recently. She did everything expected of a soldier and kept herself hidden well. If she had not slipped tonight…"

His words trailed off as he glanced back at Rebecca, now chatting casually with John by the fire, her posture relaxed as if nothing had happened.

Thomas watched her too, an intrigued smile crossing his face. "That is quite something. Hiding in plain sight, enduring everything the rest of us do. She must have her reasons."

"She does," Wales replied. "But I don't know what they are."

Thomas's mouth curled into a faint smile. "Interesting. And how do you intend to manage this, Wales?"

Wales hesitated, the weight of the situation pressing on him. "I'll protect her as best I can."

Thomas let out a sigh, rubbing his chin. "Sometimes an opportunity appears when you least expect it."

Wales felt a flash of dread. "What do you mean?"

"My friend, we're at war," Thomas said, his voice dropping to a conspiratorial tone. "We are spying for Aunt Todd, and you know she is not particular about who she uses to get results. Men or women—it does not matter to her."

"What are you suggesting?" Wales asked, his stomach sinking.

Thomas leaned in. "She showed she can hide in plain sight. Imagine if she could slip through enemy lines. Who would suspect her?"

"That's not the point," Wales said, struggling to keep his voice steady. "It is one thing for her to be here, hidden among us. But sending her into enemy territory? If she is discovered—"

"She's the perfect candidate," Thomas pressed, his tone unwavering. "No one would suspect her. She could move through their lines, gather intelligence, and return without raising alarms."

Wales's frustration mounted, his fists clenching. "It is too dangerous. She would be walking straight into enemy hands. We can find someone else."

"Someone else?" Thomas scoffed. "Who could do what she has done? If the canal project fails, Grant will order the siege of Vicksburg. We need every advantage we can get."

Wales opened his mouth to argue, but Thomas cut him off, his tone softening, almost persuasive. "I know you're worried but think about it. The information she could bring back might turn the tide of this campaign. We cannot pass up an opportunity like this because of fear."

Wales's mind raced. Thomas had a point. Rebecca had shown resilience and courage beyond expectation, and the potential to gain from such a mission was undeniable. But her walking into such danger twisted his gut.

"And what if she's caught?" Wales whispered, his voice barely audible. "What then?"

Thomas placed a hand on his shoulder. "We are all risking our lives every day. The stakes are high, but she knows that risk. She took it when she put on that uniform."

Wales glanced over at Rebecca, watching her in the flickering light of the fire. Shadows danced across her face, illuminating a strength he had not understood until now.

As March dragged on, the men of the 95th grew discouraged. The canal project, once a symbol of hope, now seemed a lost cause. With each passing day, the rising river threatened to undo their work, eroding both the levees and their spirits. When news came on March 9th that they abandoned the project, the soldiers drained of energy, and a heavy silence hung over the camp.

As the men dispersed, Wales found Rebecca standing at the edge of the waterlogged canal, fists clenched in frustration. Her disguise held despite the toll of the grueling project, but he could see the exhaustion etched into her features. She turned as he approached, her face mirroring the frustration he felt.

"It's a hard blow," Her voice sounding rough with fatigue and disappointment.

Wales looked out at the flooded worksite; his expression grim. "We poured everything into this canal, and for what? To watch it drown under the river's weight. Half the men are sick, some are dying. It feels like we are losing without even facing the enemy."

Rebecca placed a hand on his shoulder, an intimate gesture that sent a jolt through him. He fought the urge to reach out, to pull her close and anchor himself in her presence. But beneath that longing was an anger he could not shake—anger at the risk she'd taken, at the position she'd put them both in.

"We've lost this fight," she said, "but not the war. There is still more to do, more we can accomplish."

Wales sighed, glancing away as he wrestled with the turmoil inside him. "Yes. And your part in this will be grander than you realize."

Unable to bear the intensity of the moment, he turned and walked away, leaving her standing alone by the abandoned canal, her figure outlined against the fading light. The tension between them hung in the air, unresolved and simmering, as he wondered how much longer he could keep his anger—and his heart—under control.

Chapter Seven

Crouching low in the tall brush along a creek bed, Rebecca tightened the bindings around her chest, securing her disguise with practiced precision. She embodied the role of Albert Cashin so completely—or so she hoped. She moved like Albert, spoke like him, a soldier blending into the 95th by necessity and sheer determination.

After a grueling day of hauling supplies and preparing meals, Rebecca seized a rare chance to slip away from camp unnoticed. Dinner had been a hearty stew made with vegetables from a sympathetic sutler, and the men, well-fed for once, relaxed around the fire. While they filled tin cups and swapped stories, she disappeared into the night, heading down to the creek side.

The water mirrored the gray sky, rippling under a light breeze that stirred the thick, humid air. Damp vegetation and rich, loamy earth created a heavy, earthy scent as Rebecca found a secluded spot among the trees. Alone at last, she exhaled, loosening the bindings with relief. The day's labor had made them tight, each breath a constant reminder of the deception encasing her like armor. She took a deep breath, savoring a brief reprieve from the strict confines of her disguise.

A sudden crack in the thicket snapped her attention. She crouched lower, heart pounding, scanning the dense undergrowth. But then she spotted the source of the noise—a small bird hopping along the water's edge, oblivious to her as it pecked at the soil for insects. Rebecca let out a quiet sigh, her own skittishness bringing a reluctant smile.

As she readjusted the bindings, thoughts drifted to Samuel Peppers. Kindhearted and easygoing, Samuel accepted her presence without question or suspicion. He treated her just as he did any other soldier, and she found solace in his company. But the fear of his discovering her secret troubled her. How would he react? Would he feel deceived or betrayed, or show understanding? She pushed the thought aside—some truths needed to stay buried.

Yet Samuel's acceptance was not the only weight pressing on her. Since Wales had uncovered her secret, he had kept a deliberate distance, leaving her caught between anger and hurt. She had known her presence would shock him, but his cold, almost calculating silence unsettled her more than she wanted to admit. Every sidelong glance, every time he seemed about to speak to change his mind, reinforced the feeling that he saw her as a burden, a problem best left unsolved. His rejection cut deeply, exposing vulnerabilities she had left behind in New York. She did not know how to bridge the widening chasm, how to find the words that might ease the unspoken tension between them. His silence felt like condemnation, leaving her feeling more alone than ever since donning the uniform.

With the bindings secured again, she pulled on her wool shirt, tucking it into her trousers, then slipped her jacket back on. Hints of spring had showed, warmer days offering a small comfort amid the harshness of camp life. Bracing against the cool evening air, she made her way back toward camp.

Her mind wandered over the past few weeks— the grueling march to Lake Providence, the endless, backbreaking labor on the canal. General Grant had pinned his hopes on this canal to bypass Vicksburg, but nature had betrayed them. The river, relentless and unyielding, washed away their efforts, leaving the men with weary bodies and defeated spirits.

Collaborating with John Scobell and Samuel, she had spent countless days hauling tree limbs and clearing debris, muscles aching from the strain. The physical toll of the work felt harsh enough, but the emotional weight pressed down even harder. And always there was Wales—his avoidance, his silence, his refusal to meet her eyes for more than a fleeting moment. Did he see her as a burden, a mistake he wished he could erase? Or, as she feared, did he view her presence as a liability?

The unknown gnawed at her, unsettling her more than the grind of camp life. She had defied so many odds to reach this point. His unspoken rejection weighed in the air between them, an ever-present discomfort that she could not ignore, no matter how hard she tried.

As she approached camp, a sentry waved her through, and the familiar sounds of soldiers settling in for the night surrounded her—the low murmur of conversation, the crackling of firewood, the clinking of tin cups. Samuel's familiar snores drifted from their tent, a comforting rhythm amid the quiet.

But even in the familiarity of camp, unease lingered. She moved among the brotherhood of soldiers, yet somehow remained apart. She had faced danger and struggled beside them, but uncertainty loomed, casting shadows over her purpose. With Wales's rejection lingering like a bruise, her resolve wavered.

*   *   *

Rebecca sat by the dying embers of the campfire, letting its fading warmth seep into her weary bones. Shadows from the flickering flames stretched long across the ground, casting an illusion of solitude. Then, without warning, Corporal Thomas Humphrey appeared beside her, breaking the quiet.

Why is he here? She lowered her hand to the ground, feeling for a rock or stick to defend herself if needed. Had he seen something? Had she slipped up? Her mind raced, searching for reasons for his presence, weighing every option for escape.

After what felt like an eternity, Thomas broke the silence, his voice low, each word carrying an unmistakable weight that made her heart pound.

"Albert," he began, pausing, his tone cold and deliberate. "Or rather…Rebecca."

The world seemed to tilt as his words struck. Her blood froze; the murmurs of the campfire and distant sounds of camp faded into nothing. Her heartbeat thundered in her ears, fear tightening her throat.

"Don't look so surprised," Thomas said, his gaze steady and unyielding. "I've known for a while now."

Rebecca's pulse quickened, confusion and alarm tangling within her. "How?" she whispered. "How did you find out?"

Thomas's mouth twisted in a faint, almost admiring smile. "You are good, Rebecca. Particularly good. But not perfect. The day you caught that crate on the wagon—it gave me my first clue. Then Wales told me your name. I have seen people hide in plain sight before. It is difficult."

He raised a hand, sensing her fear. "Calm down. I am not here to expose you. Quite the opposite. You have done well with the ruse, and that is why we need you."

Rebecca's brow knit in confusion. "You need me. For what? Who else knows?"

Thomas leaned closer, lowering his voice to a near whisper. "John, Wales, and I—we are not just soldiers or camp cooks. We are spies, gathering intelligence, passing information to those who need it. And now, we want you to join us."

His words hit her like cannon fire. Wales, a spy. She had thought him just another soldier, a reprieve from her past. Covert operations felt surreal, like the tales she had heard in whispers back home. Now they wanted her to enter this world of shadows and secrets.

"Why me?" she asked, suspicion lacing her tone.

"Because no one else could do what you've done," Thomas replied, his gaze unwavering. "You have lived among us, hidden in plain sight, and no one suspected a thing. That takes skill, cunning, and courage—the exact traits we need for the mission we are planning."

Rebecca swallowed, her mind racing. "What mission?"

"We need someone to infiltrate Jackson, Mississippi," Thomas explained. "The Confederates have fortified the city, and we need to know their plans, their defenses, and their weak points. You can get in where others cannot. As a woman, the Confederates will not see you as a threat. If you can gather that intelligence, it might be the edge we need to turn the tide in this war."

Her mind swirled, his proposition settling on her shoulders. She had never imagined herself as a spy, let alone one tasked with infiltrating enemy lines. Navigating Jackson's streets, each turn a potential discovery, sent a chill through her. Yet beneath the dread, she felt a strange sense of purpose.

Thomas sensed her hesitation and leaned in, his voice growing more intense. "Rebecca, either we acknowledge the 'C.S.A.' as a separate nation, or we conquer them completely. But to conquer them, we must make war—and not just skirmishes or battles, but total war. Destruction and desolation, suffering inflicted on the innocent and the guilty. This war must involve plundering, burning, killing, everything that makes it impossible for them to rise against us again." His words cut through the night, dark and resolute. "This country has never felt the same horror that they've inflicted on others, and that's what it will take to make them understand."

She stared at him, the weight of his words settling like iron in her chest.

"If we have any hope of sparing them—or ourselves—from more bloodshed, then we need intelligence, strategy, insight that can change the course of this fight," he continued. "Your help could mean sparing some of that suffering. Information, not just guns and soldiers, could save lives—on both sides. That is why we need you, Rebecca."

Her pulse quickened again, this time not from fear but from the growing reality of what he was asking. Her disguise, her deception—it could become something more, something that might impact not just her life, but the lives of thousands.

"And if I refuse?" she asked, her voice tight.

Thomas paused, letting the question linger, unspoken consequences hanging between them. When he spoke, his calm tone sent a shiver down her spine.

"You could refuse, but then what? Return to camp, keep digging trenches, hauling debris, hearing for the day someone else figures out your secret? You have done well, but time frays all disguises. What happens when someone else figures it out?"

He let the question hang, the weight of it pressing on her.

"If you refuse," he continued, "you go back to living as Albert, always looking over your shoulder, wondering who might be next to discover the truth. But if you accept, you become more than a soldier hiding in plain sight. You gain a purpose—one that could change the course of this war. President Lincoln himself said that Vicksburg is the key to victory—the war cannot end until that key lies in our hands."

His words hung in the air, the choice he offered feeling like a path that could go one way.

"I won't force you, Rebecca," Thomas added, his tone softer. "But you are the best person for this mission, and you know it. If you refuse, I will not hold it against you. But remember, this war is not only fought on the battlefield. It is fought in shadows; in places most soldiers cannot reach. You have already proven you can survive in those shadows."

Thomas leaned closer, his eyes locking onto hers. "The choice is yours. But keep in mind, the safest place to might be the one where you hold control, where you serve a purpose. Out there, as a spy, you gain that control. You decide your own fate."

A lump formed in her throat as she absorbed the reality before her. Thomas offered a path forward, a way to use her disguise for something greater. But his unspoken warning remained: refusing meant a life spent hiding, each day holding the threat of discovery.

As the fire crackled and the night settled around them, Rebecca realized that while Thomas had presented her with a choice, he had also shown her the real path to survival.

Rebecca approached the supply wagon, took a deep breath, and steadying herself for what lay ahead. The camp lay quiet under the night sky, most soldiers already turned in for the night, leaving a few shadows moving through the darkness. She spotted

John Scobell by the wagon, his figure illuminated by the dim glow of a nearby lantern as he sorted through a crate with deliberate, unhurried movements, each gesture calm, as though time held no sway over him.

"John," she called out, checking her surroundings to ensure no one else lingered nearby.

John looked up, his calm gaze meeting hers. His expression held a knowing quality, as if he'd anticipated this moment. Without a word, he motioned for her to come closer.

Rebecca hesitated, her heart pounding as she took the final steps to close the distance. "We need to talk," Her voice barely above a whisper.

John set aside the crate and leaned against the wagon, studying her with a steady, almost expectant look. "Figured as much," he replied, his tone measured, carrying a trace of something she couldn't quite place.

Rebecca took another breath, knowing that speaking the truth would change everything. "John, there is something you should know. I am not who you think I am."

John's face did not register surprise. His gaze remained steady, a faint smile tugging at the corner of his mouth. "You're not Albert Cashin," he said, as though it were the simplest truth. "You're Rebecca."

Her breath caught, stunned by his nonchalance. She had prepared herself for shock, even anger, but not this calm, almost casual acknowledgment.

"You knew? For how long?" she asked, disbelief threading through her voice.

John nodded, his gaze steady. "A while now. Secrets do not last long in a place like this, but you have done well. Better than most."

Relief mingled with apprehension as Rebecca tried to process his reaction. "Why didn't you say anything?"

John shrugged, his expression softening. "Was not my place. We all have reasons for being here, reasons we keep hidden. Your secret was yours to hold, not mine to give away."

His words settled over her like a mantle of unexpected solidarity. For the first time, she felt a connection with John beyond their shared duties. They were both hiding, both weaving deceptions into the fabric of the camp.

Earlier that night, Corporal Humphrey had pressed her to speak with John about his "special role," hinting that John's mission might align with her own. Now, knowing John's quiet acceptance of her secret, she felt compelled to share the truth.

"Thomas told me everything," she began, her voice firmer now. "We are spies—all of us. And they have pulled me into it. Thomas and Wales… they want me to go to Jackson. They say I can help, but I am not sure I'm ready for this, John."

John's eyebrows tightened as he listened, then reached into his coat pocket, pulling out a worn leather-bound book she had seen him with before. He flipped it open to the back, revealing a list of names scrawled hastily across the pages, each name followed by a plantation name and the name of the slaveholder.

"As you know now," he said, his voice carrying a newfound gravity, "I am here for a mission of my own. While Thomas and Wales follow orders from Washington, I answer to someone different. Frederick Douglass. He sent me here to find these people," he explained, his voice steady but intense, his hand tapping the list. "These are enslaved men and women. I have come to locate them and, if I can, help them find their freedom."

Rebecca's eyes traced the names, feeling the weight of each one settle in her chest. The scope of her mission, already daunting, now grew even larger.

"What do I do if I find them?" she asked, her voice quiet, almost reverent.

John's gaze softened, his expression understanding. "You tell them, 'Uncle Douglass is on his way.' Then you get word to me. I will take care of the rest."

Rebecca nodded, a sense of resolve strengthening within her. She took out her notebook and began copying the names, the names of the plantations, and the names of the slaveholders, each one a life hidden behind lines of ink, each name a chance at freedom. The realization struck her with full force: she was not just gathering information; she was holding lives in her hands, lives that counted on her.

Once she finished, she looked up, her heart both heavy and determined. "I'll do my best," she promised, the words carrying a depth of commitment she had not felt before.

John returned her nod, his face softening with reassurance. "I know you will, Rebecca. We are in this together, and we're going to do everything we can to make a difference. Remember, every name in that book is counting on us."

As Rebecca tucked the notebook away, the list of names imprinted in her memory, the gravity of her role dawned on her. She was no longer just hiding; she was part of a cause greater than herself, a purpose as sharp and resolute as the words John had spoken. And as she turned to leave, she understood that failure was not an option—not now, not with so much at stake.

*   *   *

The next evening, Rebecca stood in the dimly lit tent, heart pounding as she faced Thomas and Wales. The lantern cast flickering light and long, wavering shadows on the canvas walls, making the small space feel close and thick with tension. She felt the intensity of their gazes, the weight of the mission pressing down on her. This was no longer a discussion; the mission lay before her, and doubt had no place here.

Thomas leaned over a rough wooden table, spreading out a map of Jackson. The parchment, worn, the edges curled from constant use. He traced his finger along the city's streets, pausing at marked locations—Confederate headquarters, supply depots, homes of known Union sympathizers.

"Here," He tapped the map, his voice laced with urgency, "is where you need to be most cautious. Confederate patrols are thickest near the Capitol building. Avoid it if you can."

Rebecca nodded, committing each detail to memory. Her mind raced with everything she needed to remember, but she forced herself to focus on the task. Distractions were not an option now.

Wales stepped forward, holding a simple yet elegant dress in his hands. It was made of soft, muted blue fabric that would blend well with the somber tones of the South in wartime. He offered it to her, his expression serious.

"You'll wear this," his voice steady but tinged with concern. "It will help you pass as a young widow. Your story is that you are from New York, looking for family in the South, displaced by the war. Keep it simple and do not give more information than necessary."

Rebecca took the dress, running her fingers over the soft fabric. Returning to the role of a woman filled her with a strange mix of relief and apprehension. She had grown used to the coarse, heavy clothes of Albert, to the security of her disguise.

Wales watched her, noticing her hesitation. His gaze softened, and he gave her a reassuring look. "You'll be fine, Rebecca. Remember, you are a widow now. Speak softly, keep your head down, and act like someone weighed down by grief. No one will look twice."

She nodded, swallowing against the tightness in her throat. After so long as Albert, she almost did not remember what it felt like to be Rebecca. But she had no time for second thoughts.

Thomas placed a small pistol in her hand, the metal cool and solid. "Keep this hidden in your reticule," he instructed. "Use it if there is no other choice. The goal is to blend in, not fight your way out."

Rebecca slipped the pistol into her small bag, feeling the cold metal as a reminder of the stakes. She looked up at Thomas, seeing the concern etched into his face. His steady gaze gave her strength.

Wales handed her a tiny vial of ink and a slender quill next. "For encoding messages," he explained. "Work it into simple notes—recipes, Bible verses, anything that wouldn't raise suspicion."

Rebecca took the vial and quill, the importance of the mission sank deeper with every item. This was more than gathering intelligence; it was stepping into a world of danger where one mistake could be fatal.

Then, Thomas glanced between her and Wales. "And your name. It is best not to use your real one. Do you have another in mind?"

Rebecca focused for a moment, an idea sparking with a glint of mischief in her eye. "Alice Strong," she replied, letting the name fall as if it were any other.

Wales's expression stiffened, his eyes widening. "Alice Strong? Of all names, that is the one you pick?"

Amusement flickered in Thomas's eyes, a barely contained smile pulling at his lips as he caught on to the name's significance. "Alice Strong… Yes, that does have a nice, resilient ring to it."

Rebecca fought to keep her face serious, but the hint of a smile crept up despite her efforts. She shrugged, feigning innocence. "It suits the mission, don't you think?"

Wales flushed, his jaw clenching. "Rebecca, I don't think you understand—"

"Oh, I understand," she said, a glint of humor in her gaze. "But it is perfect, really. Alice is a very suitable name for a young woman in this situation."

Thomas chuckled, unable to hold it back any longer. "Wales, I think it is a fine name. Besides, it will keep Rebecca in character, don't you think?"

Wales exhaled, struggling to keep his composure as he looked at both. "If anything goes wrong," he muttered, "I'll never live this down."

Rebecca slipped the locket around her neck, feeling its cool metal against her skin, a final symbol of the mission's reality. As she let the amusement settle into determination, she straightened, meeting both of their gazes.

"I won't let you down." Her voice firm despite the fear simmering beneath her resolve.

Wales gave her a tight nod, his eyes still holding traces of irritation mixed with reluctant admiration. "We know you won't," he replied. "You're ready for this… Alice."

Chapter Eight

Wales stood by the riverbank, his eyes never leaving Rebecca as she took the bundle of women's clothes he'd handed her. The air between them charged, the weight of the mission pressing down on them both. She had to go as herself, as Rebecca, but shedding the disguise of Albert felt far too personal, far too vulnerable.

As she climbed into the back of the supply wagon, disappearing behind the canvas flaps, Wales took a step back to grant her privacy. Every faint rustle of fabric, every quiet shift, stirred emotions he struggled to control. This was Rebecca, not Albert—the woman he had once known and left behind, and now she was about to walk straight into danger. When he heard the soft parting of the canvas, he turned, heart pounding, as she stepped out.

She stood before him, no longer disguised as Albert but as herself, her hair pinned beneath a blue cap, a stray curl framing her face. She was different, yet achingly familiar, a reminder of everything he had tried to leave behind. In her hand, she held out a small, folded square of fabric—his handkerchief.

Wales blinked, his chest tightening with the realization that she had kept it, carried it with her all this time.

"Strange, isn't it?" she said, glancing down at the handkerchief before meeting his gaze. "Seeing me like this again."

He swallowed, struggling for words. "It is," he managed, his voice thick. "But…it suits you. This is who you are."

Her eyes softened, a faint smile crossed her lips as she looked down at the handkerchief, her thumb brushed its edge before she looked back at him. "You thought I'd forgotten about you… about this. But I did not. I never forgot."

His breath caught, and he reached out, letting his fingers rested the handkerchief in her hand before letting his hand drift up, resting on her shoulder. She stepped close enough so he could feel the warmth of her presence, the faint scent of apple on her. Her gaze held a quiet strength and a courage he had admired in her all along.

"Rebecca…" he said, his voice a rough whisper, his hand lingering on her shoulder. But he held back, reigning in his feelings as the weight of her mission settled on him. He cleared his throat, willing his voice to steady. "This is your first mission. Do nothing that will draw attention to yourself. Just…get the information and get out. Understand?"

She nodded, her gaze steady as she took in his words. Wales exhaled, the tension in his chest eased, though he could not shake the worry gnawing at him. He knew the danger she was walking into, but she had to be careful, had to stay hidden and quick.

"We know there's a single railroad linking Jackson to Vicksburg," he continued, his voice low. "But what we do not know is their plan to use it. Do they have reinforcements coming? How far away is General Joseph Johnston? And if you can, find out if anyone knows what General Pemberton's plans are for Vicksburg—the town Grant is set on taking. That is all. Get in, find what you can, and get out."

Rebecca met his gaze, her eyes filled with determination. "I understand," she said, her voice soft yet unwavering.

He wanted to say more, wanted to reach for her, pull her close, and tell her to be safe. He rested a hand on her arm, his touch lingering, silent support in a world full of noise. "Be careful, Rebecca."

A figure stepped out of the shadows at the river's edge, and Wales pulled away. "This is Daniel," he said, forcing himself to focus. "One of John's connections. He will take you across the river and escort you to the outskirts of Jackson. And when you are ready to leave, he'll get you back to us."

Daniel nodded, stepping forward to take her carpet bag with a respectful nod. "Yes, Miss, we'll get you there safe."

Rebecca glanced back at Wales, a question and a promise in her eyes. He nodded, giving her a final, steady look. She turned and followed Daniel down the path to the river; her figure receding but not disappearing from his mind. She carried his handkerchief—and his hopes for her safe return.

As she disappeared into the distance, Wales felt a surge of protectiveness and something more—a deep, unspoken longing. He could hope that the woman he had known as both Albert and Rebecca, the woman now carrying his heart with her, would return to him. Mission be damned.

*   *   *

The next day Wales Wood stood at the edge of Lake Providence, staring out at the shimmering water under the first light of dawn. The air hung thick with humidity, already clinging to his skin, and he knew it would be another grueling day under the relentless

Southern sun. Around him, the camp of the 95th Illinois stirred with life, soldiers preparing for their next march. The orders were clear: they would join the campaign moving closer to Vicksburg, passing through Richmond, Louisiana, to join other regiments at Smith's Plantation near Milliken's Bend.

But this campaign felt different, and there was a tension in the air that Wales could not ignore. The entire regiment seemed on edge, as if each man sensed they were being drawn into something far greater— and far deadlier—than anything they had faced so far.

Wales's attention drifted to Corporal Thomas Humphery, who was in deep conversation with a wiry stranger who seemed to materialize from the shadows. Thomas had countless connections, people he trusted to pass information from one side of enemy lines to the other. Wales knew these were not idle talks—every word exchanged with these men brought critical information about Confederate troop movements, hidden artillery, and the location of snipers. They were deep into rebel territory now, and every crack of gunfire in the distance reminded them of the risk. No one could tell whether the shots came from Confederate soldiers, hidden sympathizers, or locals caught in the war's sweep.

Thomas caught Wales's gaze and nodded, a silent signal that his work was done—for now. Wales had his own task to fulfill: Thomas had given him a collection of special dispatches to send, messages filled with strange phrases and unusual spellings that meant little to him but everything to those who could decipher them. Wales managed the cryptic dispatches while knowing Aunt Todd trusted most Thomas—their covert contact, hidden behind Union lines, who passed vital intelligence to them. Aunt Todd's trust in Thomas was absolute, and Wales could see why; Thomas's knowledge, skill, and calm were the linchpins that held their delicate network together.

With a final glance, Thomas nodded and stepped back, disappearing into the bustle of camp. Wales tucked the dispatches into his pocket, glancing around at the camp as it buzzed with the rhythm of packing and preparing for the march.

The road to Milliken's Bend was brutal. The sun blazed overhead, turning the dusty path into a blistering furnace. Wales's uniform clung to his back, soaked with sweat, and his boots chafed his feet raw. He saw the exhaustion etched into the faces of the surrounding soldiers, each step an effort, yet not a single complaint crossed their lips. They pushed forward in grim silence, driven by duty and determination.

By the time they reached Smith's Plantation, the scene was one of decay and ruin, far from any grandeur it might once have known. The grand house stood hollow, its walls scarred by war, and vines crept up through cracks, as if nature herself sought to reclaim it. The plantation, transformed into a military camp, and the 95th Illinois, found themselves assigned to General Ransom's brigade, the 6th Division, 17th Army Corps.

The place was heavy with history and stories untold. Wales wandered the grounds, drifted to the lives that must have been lived here, disrupted and twisted by the force of war. The plantation's decaying structures and silent fields seemed to resisted their presence, as if the land itself remembered.

The sweltering heat grew unbearable by late afternoon. Wales noticed a small pond at the plantation's edge, its water shimmering in the golden light. Some men, their shirts already soaked through, cooled offed, splashing, and laughing as they swam, escaping the grim reality of war.

But the reprieve shattered in an instant. A panicked cry rang out as one man thrashed in the water; his face contorted in pain. The others realized he was not playing around—something was very wrong. Wales's heart leapt into his throat as he recognized the soldier: Samuel Peppers. Wales bolted toward the pond, pulling off his boots as he ran.

Diving into the water, Wales felt the coolness of the pond shock his overheated skin, but there was no time to savor it. He swam toward Samuel, grabbing him by the arms and hauling him toward shore. The others helped drag him out, laying him on the ground as he gasped for breath, his face pale and shivering.

It was then that Wales saw the two puncture marks on Samuel's calf, blood trickling from the wounds, the flesh already beginning to swell. The realization hit him like a blow—a water moccasin, venomous and deadly, had bitten Samuel in the pond.

Wales acted fast, his voice calm despite his concern. "Get the surgeon!" he shouted, watching as a soldier ran to fetch help. Wales knelt beside Samuel, gripping his hand to offer reassurance.

"What was that thing? Am I…am I gonna make it?" Samuel's voice shook, fear stark in his eyes. "I didn't go through all this to die by a snake!"

"You're not going to die," Wales said, his tone steady. "You have survived this far. You will make it through this too."

Wales stayed by his side, murmuring words of comfort he was not sure would be enough. Finally, the surgeon arrived, his face grim as he examined the wound, and John Scobell followed close behind, carrying a canvas stretcher.

"We need to get the venom out," the surgeon said, his voice tight. "Hold him down."

"He's right," John added. "I am from these parts. Those snakes are nasty—gotta move quick."

Together, Wales and the others held Samuel down as the surgeon worked. Wales averted his gaze as the surgeon cut into the wound to drain the venom, Samuel's agonized screams echoing through the camp. When the surgeon finished, Samuel was weak and barely conscious.

They rolled him onto the stretcher, carrying him to a makeshift infirmary in camp. Wales and John volunteered to stay by his side through the night, determined to keep watch until they were certain he was stable. The plantation, once eerie, now felt downright hostile, as if it held a grudge against their presence.

As night fell, the camp settled into an uneasy silence. The day's events had shaken the men, a harsh reminder that the dangers of war were not limited to the battlefield. Wales sat outside the infirmary, his mind heavy with Samuel's care and the ever-present gunfire echoing in the distance. This land was rebel territory, with dangers at every turn.

By dawn, Samuel was still alive, though his recovery would be slow. Wales knew the march would continue soon, drawing them deeper into Confederate territory, toward Vicksburg and the heart of the fight. But Smith's Plantation had left a mark on him, a reminder that survival in war required more than courage; it demanded vigilance and resilience against the unexpected. And as Wales stood with the morning sun casting its light over the camp, he felt a renewed determination to see them throughout to the other side—no matter what dangers lay ahead.

*　　*　　*

Wales charged forward, his heart pounding in his chest, his boots pounding against the dry, cracked ground as the men of the 95th Illinois surged toward the Confederate earthworks. In a few days, they travelled from the easy camp at the plantation to where they aimed to take Vicksburg.

The air was thick with smoke and the acrid smell of gunpowder, mingling with the oppressive heat. His rifle was heavy in his hands, each step feeling like a march into hell itself. All around him, the shouts of officers, the screams of wounded men, and the deafening blasts of cannon fire filled the air, a symphony of chaos that swallowed everything.

Ahead, Vicksburg's defenses loomed like walls of a fortress, the Confederate earthworks towering, bristling with artillery and lined with enemy soldiers. The Union artillery had pounded these positions for days, yet the defenses held firm, as menacing and impenetrable as ever. Wales felt a shiver of fear, replaced by the iron resolve that kept him moving forward. There was no turning back now.

A shell exploded to his right, sending dirt, rock, and fragments of shattered bodies into the air. Wales flinched, shielding his face, feeling the sharp sting of debris cutting into his skin. When he looked up, the man beside him—a young soldier he had not learned the name of—lay on the ground, his body torn open, blood pooling around him in the dirt. Wales swallowed hard, pushing down the surge of nausea and horror. He could not stop; stopping meant death.

The Union line pressed on, men falling with every step as Confederate bullets ripped through their ranks. Wales felt the eerie sensation of a bullet whizzing past his ear, close enough that he could feel the air shift as it missed him by inches. The man just behind him was not as lucky; a sharp crack rang out, and he went down with a strangled cry, his face twisted in agony as he clutched his bleeding shoulder.

"Keep moving!" Wales shouted to the men around him, his voice hoarse, barely audible over the noise. He forced himself forward, his boots slipping in the blood-soaked mud, his senses heightened to every sound, every movement. Ahead, the Confederate soldiers fired, their faces shadowed beneath their hats, but he could see the flashes of grim determination, the set jaws, the hardened eyes of men defending their ground.

The Union soldiers fell in droves, each step forward paid for in blood. Wales's lungs burned with every breath, the smoke choking him, his vision blurred by sweat and tears he could not afford to wipe away. He stumbled over the body of a fallen comrade, his boot slipping in the man's blood, almost sending him sprawling. He gritted his teeth, righting himself, and forced his legs to keep moving.

To his left, he saw a man from his company—Private O'Connor—go down, clutching his abdomen as dark blood seeped between his fingers. His face was pale, his eyes wide with shock, and Wales could see the awful realization dawning in them. There was no saving him. The look of horror etched on

O'Connor's face would haunt Wales for the rest of his life.

Wales fought the urge to look away as more men fell around him. Each loss felt like a physical blow, each scream embedding itself into his memory. He barely had time to process it all as he pressed on, his own survival the thing keeping him grounded. The noise was relentless, the blasts of artillery shaking the ground beneath him, sending tremors through his body as he advanced.

Suddenly, the man ahead of him took a bullet to the side of his throat, his eyes widening in shock as blood sprayed from his wound. He collapsed, his hands clawing at his neck in a futile attempt to stem the flow. Wales stepped around him, his stomach twisting, but he forced himself to focus. The earthworks were closer now, the Confederate soldiers firing from above with deadly precision; cutting down Union men in waves.

Wales's hands were slick with sweat as he raised his rifle, taking aim at one of the Confederate soldiers in the trench. His heart pounded as he squeezed the trigger, the recoil jarring him as he watched the man fall back, clutching his chest where Wales's bullet had struck. But there was no time for satisfaction or remorse; another man took the fallen soldier's place almost immediately, and Wales knew he was just one small part of this vast, merciless machine.

An explosion erupted nearby, sending shrapnel flying. Wales felt a hot, searing pain in his leg as a fragment sliced through his pants, cutting into his flesh. He stumbled, a sharp gasp escaped him, but he pushed on, gritting his teeth against the pain. Around him, the screams of the wounded mingled with the thunder of cannon fire, each cry a testament to the brutality of this battle.

The Union line faltered as men began to fall back, unable to withstand the relentless barrage. Wales found himself pressed up against a cluster of his fellow soldiers, their faces pale and streaked with dirt and blood, eyes wide with the dawning horror of what they were facing. Men shouted for retreat, others fired blindly, desperate to push forward despite the overwhelming odds.

Wales's own voice joined the clamor, urging those around him to hold the line, though he could feel the futility in his words. Every second felt like an eternity, each heartbeat a countdown to his own end. He fired his rifle repeatedly, reloading with shaking hands, his every movement driven by instinct and training as he fought to survive.

Finally, a Union officer's voice cut through the chaos, shouting the order to fall back. Wales's relief was both tempered by the weight of failure and the horror of what he had just witnessed. He turned, retreating with the others, his steps heavy with exhaustion and pain. Around him, the ground littered with bodies—men he had marched besides, shared rations with, laughed with, now lay broken and silent.

As he stumbled away from the Confederate lines, Wales felt an overwhelming sense of dread settle over him. They had come so far, fought so hard, only to be met with devastation. The sight of Vicksburg's earthworks, still standing, unyielding and defiant, was a cruel reminder of the brutal fight ahead. And though he had survived the day, he knew this was just the beginning of battle.

Chapter Nine

Rebecca took a steady breath. She was no longer Albert Cashin, a woman hidden behind a soldier's facade; she was a Union spy, slipping into hostile territory on a mission that could tip the scales of the battle for Vicksburg.

The sky had begun its slow descent into dusk, casting long shadows across the dirt path leading to Jackson, Mississippi. Rebecca, now clothed in the modest dark blue mourning attire of a Southern widow, kept her head bowed. The wide brim of her hat shrouded her face, shielding her features from the rare passerby while blending her into the rural landscape. The sounds breaking the silence were the occasional rumble of distant artillery fire and the murmur of leaves stirred by a faint breeze.

Rebecca sat on the supply wagon beside Daniel, her modest blue dress blending just enough to avoid unwanted attention but distinguishing her from the enslaved man driving the wagon. Daniel's face remained steady as they neared the gates of Jackson. This was not just a casual journey; they'd agreed on a careful backstory that would hold up under scrutiny.

With Federal soldiers rumored to be pushing closer every day, towns and roads were becoming less safe, and Daniel's owner had ordered him to take her into town for her own security.

"Keep quiet and let me do the talking," Daniel advised in a low tone as they approached the city gates, his gaze fixed ahead.

Rebecca gave a slight nod, keeping her hands folded in her lap. She held her head at a modest angle, black bonnet shading her face, and kept her eyes on the ground as they approached the sentries.

The road, crowded with soldiers and supply wagons, the air thick with dust and tension. Confederate guards patrolled the gates, inspecting each wagon that passed through. As Daniel slowed the mules, he raised his hand in a practiced gesture to greet a nearby sentry.

"Supply run from Master Harland's plantation," Daniel announced, his tone even. "Brought this woman into town, sir, by orders of the master—too risky out there for her with all the Yankees about."

The guard glanced over the crates of supplies, then gave Rebecca a brief, disinterested look, his attention caught more by the goods in the wagon than by her presence.

"Who is she to him?" the guard asked, eyeing her with passing curiosity.

"Just a widow woman needing to find kin in Jackson," Daniel replied. "Master wanted her safe in town, not on the road alone."

The guard grunted, satisfied with the explanation, and waved them through with a quick nod. Rebecca let out the breath she had been holding, relieved to get through without further questioning.

The streets of Jackson pulsed with tension, soldiers in gray uniforms moved in clusters while civilians scurried past, their eyes averted from the military presence. War had seeped into the bones of this city; she could feel it in the hurried steps of passersby and the wary glances they exchanged.

Daniel guided the wagon toward the Magnolia House, giving her a quick nod as they approached. "It's just ahead. The housekeeper and cook will know how to look after you. They will make sure you're seen as little as possible."

Rebecca returned his nod with a grateful glance. Daniel had risked much to bring her into Jackson and set up these connections. As they reached the boardinghouse, Daniel climbed down and extended a hand, assisting her from the wagon with a respectful air, just as any loyal servant might assist a passenger.

"If you need to get word to me, leave a note under your pillow," he murmured as she stepped down. "The housekeeper will make sure it gets to me."

"Thank you, Daniel," she whispered. She watched him climb back onto the wagon, giving her a steady nod before he urged the mules forward to continue his delivery.

Rebecca turned to face the Magnolia House, taking in a deep, steadying breath. With Daniel's help and her own determination, she was ready to assume her role, slip into the fabric of Jackson's daily life, and gather the intelligence the Union needed.

∗   ∗   ∗

The city itself was a study in contrasts, alive with bustling energy yet shadowed by the toll of war. As she walked around town, she saw small groups of Confederate soldiers marching with dust-streaked gray uniforms and grim faces, while civilians hurried, eyes averted, avoiding the soldiers' glances. The signs of strain were visible in every step and lowered gaze, evidence of a city crumbling under the relentless weight of conflict.

Rebecca moved through the streets, her steps careful and deliberate, each one an act of blending in, of becoming just another anonymous face in a sea of weary faces. She kept her head low, but her ears keen, listening for any passing hints of Confederate strategy. As she neared a cluster of soldiers gathered by a tavern, she heard the low, intense murmur of conversation—just the kind she was hoping to overhear.

"I heard General Pemberton's got something big planned," muttered one soldier, his hand resting on the hilt of his sword.

"Reckon it's a new offensive," another replied, casting a wary glance around them as if expecting to see spies. "They are keeping tight-lipped about it. Could be we are moving out soon… maybe even a siege."

Pretending to adjust the shawl around her shoulders, Rebecca slowed, leaning closer to catch their words. The men paid her no mind, too engrossed in their conversation to notice.

"Whatever it is, we need to be ready," the first soldier said, his voice edged with tension. "Word is the Yankees are closing in; it's a matter of time before they make their move on Jackson."

"If we can hold Vicksburg," another added, "then maybe this will be the last year of the war. But if we lose it, well…" He trailed off, a grim silence filling the pause. "It'll be a long road to independence."

Rebecca felt a chill despite the heat. The Confederates were bracing for something big in Vicksburg. As the soldiers continued their talk, she took a step back, merging once again into the bustling streets. Her mind was racing, each piece of overheard conversation slotting into her growing understanding of their plans. Every step brought her closer to the Magnolia House, and closer to delivering the critical information the Union needed.

She filed away the information, her mind racing. Intelligence was easier to gather than she assumed. If the Confederates were planning an offensive, it could mean they were trying to break the siege or reinforce their defenses. Either way, it was crucial knowledge that needed to get back to the Union forces.

Rebecca discontinued her walk, returning to the Magnolia House to settle for the night.

*   *   *

The Magnolia House was a stately antebellum home, once grand, but now weathered by years of neglect and hardship. Towering magnolia trees shaded the expansive porch, lined with white columns that hinted at a past elegance. Inside, the house kept a charm of faded splendor: mahogany furniture worn smooth over time, drapes fraying at the edges, and a grand chandelier that, though dusty, still caught the light in delicate prisms. Rebecca could only imagine what it had looked like before the war.

When she entered, Rebecca expected the inn to be sparsely populated, perhaps hosting a few older women left behind as their husbands went off to war. She was wrong. To her surprise, well-dressed ladies filled the communal areas, some gathered in quiet conversation, others seated with an air of practiced leisure. They wore gowns of fine fabric and elegant shawls, their hair carefully arranged, exuding an aura of sophistication and resilience even as the city braced for conflict. Rebecca adjusted her modest blue dress, suddenly conscious of her own plainer attire among these Confederate ladies who seemed almost untouched by the hardships of war.

At the check-in desk, she signed the guest book under her alias, "Alice Strong," and, as rehearsed, listed her origin as New York. She did not miss the raised eyebrows from the clerk at her Northern roots, but he said nothing and handed her a key with a polite nod.

Rebecca ascended the creaking staircase, footsteps echoing in the quiet hall. At the top, a single lantern cast a dim glow, enough to guide her to her room. She slid the key into the brass lock, feeling the worn grooves as it clicked open.

The room was modest, bearing the signs of the war's toll. A small bed sat against the far wall, its wrought-iron frame chipped and rusted in places, covered with a neatly folded patchwork quilt from a bygone era. A single window overlooked the alley, its faded green curtains fraying and dotted with moth holes. In one corner stood an old wardrobe with a door ajar, while a small, oval mirror above the washstand bore cracks along its edges. The pitcher on the stand was half-full, remnants of previous guests who had washed away long journeys here.

The air held a faint scent of lavender, dried sprigs tucked into the corners to preserve a semblance of comfort. A small writing desk by the window held a candle and a quill, along with loose sheets of paper left behind—letters never sent. Rebecca struck a match, lighting the candle to cast a warm glow over the worn furnishings. For now, this room, simple and shabby, would be her refuge.

The room included supper in the downstairs dining room, once a grand double parlor now filled with mismatched tables and chairs of various shapes and sizes. As Rebecca found a seat at a small table in the back, she felt an uneasy sensation—a prickling awareness of watchful eyes and hidden dangers lurking in every shadow.

When the hopeful-looking stew served, a woman approached her table, her presence confident and her face alight with curiosity.

"I noticed you're from New York," the woman began, beaming as if Rebecca were an old friend. "I am so sorry to be forward. I read your name in the register after you signed in. Well, I had to introduce myself—I am from New York as well! Mary Webster Loughborough."

Rebecca's heart skipped at the introduction. She did not recognize the name, but New York was vast. Forcing a calm smile, she extended her hand. "It is a pleasure to meet you, Mrs. Loughborough. I am Alice. Alice Strong."

"Oh, please, call me Mary," the woman insisted with a bright, too-cheerful smile. "I will call you Alice, then—it is just so rare to meet someone from back home, all the way out here! What brings you to Jackson?" She did not pause for an answer before adding, "I thought I would be miserable here when we first arrived, but it's not so bad. Sometimes there's dancing and parties, you know? I suppose they are meant to keep our spirits up, what with the Yankees and all."

Rebecca, surprised by Mary's rapid-fire friendliness, improvised. "I'm… looking for my husband's family. He passed, and these are tough times. I could use the support."

Mary's eyes widened with sympathy, her chatter pausing for a beat. "Oh, you poor dear! That is terrible. I understand, truly." Then, leaning forward with a conspiratorial smile, she added, "I am here for similar reasons myself. My husband, Major James M. Loughborough, is a quartermaster stationed in Vicksburg, and we are newly married! Isn't that something?" She gave a proud little smile. "He likes me close, you know, so I came along. I know most wives would not do it, but we are just *so* close, and he wanted me nearby. But now I am stuck here in Jackson! Can you imagine?"

Rebecca felt a twinge of anxiety. If Mary's husband held such a position, this connection might be dangerous. Yet Mary's open, sympathetic manner—and tendency to miss cues in her eagerness—made Rebecca think that keeping her close might be helpful.

"Oh, I'm so sorry for your loss," Mary continued, undeterred, her expression solemn but her eyes bright with interest. "Loneliness is such a terrible thing, isn't it? But at least we have one another! We must keep each other going. I have been beside myself with worry since New Orleans fell, and it is getting worse with Vicksburg. Do you think Vicksburg will hold, Alice?"

Rebecca hesitated, trying to stay in character. "I'm sure it's… a difficult time for all," she said diplomatically. "It has been challenging. I was not religious before, but now I pray every day. There is so much to lose."

Mary placed a comforting hand on Rebecca's arm, missing her vagueness. "You do not have to go through this alone, Alice! I know just what you need—a party in Vicksburg! There is one coming up, just a small gathering, really, but it will lift your spirits to be around people, if only for a while. And" she added in a whisper, "You never know what you'll hear at those things, with all the men and their talk of strategy! You could even meet another soldier."

Rebecca's mind raced. Vicksburg was critical for her mission, and this invitation was an opportunity to gather intelligence. Mary's offer was risky, but her openness and chattiness suggested that she would suspect nothing unusual.

"I appreciate your kindness, Mary," she replied, forcing a grateful smile. "A change of scenery would do me good. I still have not found his family, and… well, I am not sure they're even here anymore."

"Oh, wonderful!" Mary exclaimed, her face lighting up. "We will leave tomorrow! You will see— it will do you good to meet people. You will feel right at home. And sometimes, life surprises us, even in these dark times." She leaned in with a conspiratorial wink. "My husband says the Confederacy is full of 'surprises' if you look close enough."

Rebecca smiled, keeping her nerves hidden as Mary launched into a story about a recent party in Vicksburg. She listened, gleaning what information she could. Tomorrow, she would enter the heart of enemy territory with her chatty guide, knowing Mary's presence might be the perfect shield.

That night, Rebecca lay in bed, anticipation mixing with unease. Tomorrow, with Mary's chatter as her cover, she would move deeper into her mission—and closer to the secrets held in Vicksburg.

*　　*　　*

Rebecca folded a small piece of paper and slipped it under her pillow, ensuring anyone who checked the room for a message would find it. The note was simple: "Invited to Vicksburg, will return shortly." She had paid for the room to be held for the next week—a precaution in case her return was delayed.

The next morning, she joined Mary at the train station, her heart pounding with a mix of anxiety and anticipation. Since Mary's husband was with the Confederate Army, all her expenses were covered, including companions. As they boarded the train, Rebecca forced herself to relax, slipping into the role of a woman seeking solace in her new friend's companionship.

Mary, full of energy, filled the silence with cheerful stories of her life in New York before the war and her new experiences in the South. Rebecca nodded and smiled, responding just enough to keep the conversation flowing without revealing much about herself. Soon they were laughing over shared memories of New York—the bustling streets, good coffee, theater nights, and the city's vibrant energy.

As the train rumbled closer to Vicksburg, Mary leaned in, her voice softening. "You know, Alice, I can tell you have been through a lot. But I believe there's happiness to be found, even in times like these. This party might be what you need to start fresh."

Rebecca forced a smile. She was here on a mission, and the stakes were high. But for now, she would play her part, blending in and gathering whatever information she could.

When the train pulled into the Vicksburg Station, Mary's eyes sparkled. "Welcome, Alice! Let us see what adventures await us here. And James was going to join us later tonight—oh, you will love him! He is so thoughtful. But just my luck, he was called away to help with the defenses. Isn't that just awful timing?" She paused, sweeping Rebecca along toward their destination. "But I suppose I have you, don't I?" she added with a nervous laugh.

They headed toward the home of the Dunlop family, where Mary's friends had offered them a place to stay. The house was blocks from the river and close to the defensive batteries lining the riverbanks. Rebecca could not help but note the imposing guns above and below the city, positioned along the waterfront to repel any unwanted approach. These defenses, with their heavy artillery, were formidable, and the sight confirmed why Vicksburg was so critical.

The Dunlop family welcomed them, but Rebecca barely had time to settle into her small guest room when a distant rumble shook the walls, followed by a series of deafening blasts. She froze, heart pounding, as the unmistakable sound of artillery filled the air. She rushed to the window, catching sight of bursts of light flickering on the horizon. The Union navy was making a bold move along the river, and the Confederate batteries were desperately trying to repel them.

Rebecca's pulse quickened as she watched, processing the sight before a sharp knock broke her focus. Mrs. Dunlop, a stern woman in her late forties, burst into the room, her face tight with worry. "Alice, we need to move! It is not safe here."

The sounds of artillery shook the city, as Union gunboats unleashed a relentless shelling upon Vicksburg.

Rebecca grabbed her shawl and followed Mrs. Dunlop into the hallway, where Mary was already waiting, her face pale but her chatter uninterrupted. "Did you feel that? I knew it was going to be dangerous, but this is worse than I expected! And poor James, out there somewhere, helping the soldiers." She squeezed Rebecca's arm, as if to reassure herself. "Oh, I just hope he is safe. I always knew he had to be brave but seeing it with my own eyes! Isn't it just terrifying?"

Rebecca, barely able to answer, nodded as Mary's nervous babbling filled the silence. They moved outside into the chaos, the air thick with the smell of gunpowder, while explosions echoed across the riverfront.

"Hurry!" Mary urged, her voice louder to cut through the noise as they scrambled toward a hill where several caves were dug to shelter the town's women and children. As they ran, Mary's chatter became even faster, tumbling out in a rush of words. "I was hoping to show you the best parts of Vicksburg, but this is not it. Oh, I am sure this cave is terrible—I always seen myself in Vicksburg sipping tea, but here I am running for my life!"

Rebecca managed to keep pace with her as they reached the cave entrance, dodging debris and the distant flash of shells bursting overhead. As they ducked inside, Mary kept talking, her words tripping over one another in her fear.

"Isn't this dreadful?" She clutched Rebecca's arm as they settled in among the other women. "I did not think it would be this bad when James brought me down here. He promised I'd be safe. Oh, he would hate to see me like this! And he is out there—what if he's in danger?" Mary's voice broke, but she forced a shaky smile, her fingers gripping Rebecca's arm. "But at least I have you, Alice."

Rebecca's gaze shifted around the cave, taking in the towering crates of food stacked against the walls. They were filled with dried goods, preserved meats, grains—supplies enough to withstand a prolonged siege.

Forcing her voice to remain casual, she murmured, "There is so much food here. Is all of this… for the townspeople?"

"Oh yes, my husband told me about these caves," Mary said, her tone brightening as she launched into another flood of information. "They have hundreds of these stockpiled throughout the city! Isn't that something? James says that if Jackson falls, they will all come here and hold Vicksburg to the end. You would think there is enough food to last forever!" Her laughter was nervous, a quick trill that gave away her fear despite her attempts to brush it off. "We're so lucky to have these supplies, but I'm just glad we made it here, aren't you?"

Rebecca forced a nod, absorbing the details. These Confederate preparations were more extensive than she had realized—valuable intelligence she could share if she made it back to Union lines.

The shelling continued for hours, shaking the cave with each blast. Mary's voice occasionally filled the lulls, her nervous chatter both a comfort and a distraction to those around her. "I just know James would say something comforting if he were here. He has such a way with words. Do you think he is all right? Oh, but I must not think that way! I need to be strong for him." She spoke rapidly, gripping Rebecca's hand as if she could hold her fears at bay through sheer will.

At last, the shelling subsided, and a man appeared at the entrance, his face weary but relieved. "It's safe to come out," he announced.

Rebecca followed the others into the open air, blinking as her eyes adjusted to the moonlight. The streets were eerily silent, the fires in the distance had died down. Although she kept her emotions hidden, the sight of the Union iron-clad ship passing Vicksburg filled her with renewed determination. This was why she was here, risking everything.

As they returned to the Dunlop house, Mary squeezed Rebecca's arm with urgency. "Alice, we need to leave Vicksburg. The fighting will only get worse!"

Rebecca gathered her things, her pulse still racing from the night's events. As they hurried to the edge of town, Mary continued, her voice breathless. "I know we planned to stay longer, but really, it is too dangerous! And the train is not even stopping at the depot—they're picking us up further down, where everyone's waiting."

When their carriage reached the packed train, joining the anxious passengers already seated. But just as they were leaving, the train stopped at another depot to load freight. Mary gripped Rebecca's arm, her words tumbling out in rapid succession as the shelling resumed above. "Why are they stopping now? It is madness! Oh, I knew we should have left sooner—what if something happens?"

Rebecca managed a calm response, hoping to steady Mary's nerves, but inside she was just as tense. The train shook as explosions echoed above, each blast rattling the windows. Finally, after what felt like an eternity, the train reversed direction, heading back toward safety. Relief washed over the passengers, and Mary leaned her head back, exhaling.

The journey back to Jackson felt far longer than it was. As they disembarked, Mary turned to Rebecca, her voice quieter now. "Thank heavens that is over, but I'm glad you were here with me. I do not think I could have handled it alone." Mary then embraced Rebecca in a deep hug.

Rebecca, equally exhausted, hugged her back and then nodded when their eyes met. She's narrowly escaped danger, but she had gained critical insights. This was the beginning, and she was determined to see her mission through, no matter how many risks it took.

*   *   *

As Rebecca and Mary returned to the hotel in Jackson, Rebecca approached the front desk, where the clerk handed her a small, folded note. She opened it discreetly and scanned the message. It was from Thomas, checking on her progress and the information she had gathered in Vicksburg.

Turning back to Mary, Rebecca kept her expression neutral and smiled. "It's from an acquaintance of my late husband," she explained. "He heard I was in Jackson and wanted to pass along news I might want to know. I will have to leave tomorrow to address a few matters."

Mary's face fell, but she recovered and took Rebecca's hands in hers. "Oh, Alice, I will miss you! But I understand. Before you go, please take my contact information." She scribbled an address on a piece of paper and handed it to Rebecca. "If you are ever in need, please reach out. My husband is still needed in Vicksburg, and it looks like I will soon join him, so he can watch out for me."

Rebecca hesitated, frowning. "Are you sure that is wise? Vicksburg is not safe."

Mary's smile wavered, but she nodded. "It is what he wants, and I trust him. We will get through this, Alice. And you—take care of yourself wherever you are headed."

Rebecca forced a smile, pocketing the address. "You too, Mary. Thank you for everything."

As they parted, an uneasy feeling settled in Rebecca's chest. Mary's decision to return to Vicksburg felt like a mistake, but Rebecca had her own mission to complete and could not afford distractions. She promised herself she would remember Mary's kindness and keep her in her thoughts as she moved forward.

Once alone in her room, Rebecca sat at the small writing desk by the window. Taking a deep breath, she retrieved a piece of paper and began writing down all the key details she had observed in Jackson and Vicksburg—the formidable defenses along the riverbanks, the heavy artillery ready to protect the city, and the stockpiled supplies hidden in the caves. She included notes on the Confederate troops' morale, the ironclad's attempt to slip past Vicksburg's guns, and the general atmosphere of anxiety among the civilians.

By the time she finished, the paper filled with notes she knew would be vital to the Union's strategy. She folded it and hid it in her belongings, knowing Daniel would be there by noon the next day to pick her up. With everything in order, she lay down, her mind racing with the dangers that lay ahead and the weight of the information she now carried.

Chapter Ten

Wales paced back and forth; his heart heavy with worry as the sounds of battle echoed through the camp as they tried to take Vicksburg. The sky darkened, casting long shadows across the tents, and each minute stretched endlessly, amplifying the tension wrapped around his chest. John Scobell had just delivered word through his network—Rebecca and Daniel had made it out of Jackson and were on their way back. But with the surrounding fighting intensifying, he feared they might get caught in the crossfire.

The sound of hurried footsteps interrupted him. He turned, and his breath caught when he saw her. Rebecca, disguised once again as Albert Cashin, walked into camp, her posture steady, yet marked by a weariness that betrayed her exhaustion. She looked like she had been through hell, still she had a resolve in her steps.

Wales did not think. His body moved before his mind could catch up. He strode toward her, and as he reached her, he hesitated. The sight of her in this moment—a woman he cared for, hidden behind the mask of Albert—felt strangely out of place, but his emotions were too strong to restrain. Without a word, he pulled her into a tight embrace, holding her as though he feared she might disappear once more.

"I thought I'd lost you," he whispered, his voice thick with emotion. His lips brushed her forehead, a gesture so gentle it surprised even him.

Rebecca stiffened for a moment, shocked by the sudden intimacy, but gradually relaxed in his arms. "You did not, Wales. I am here," she murmured, her voice soft but laced with a mix of exhaustion and relief.

Wales pulled back just enough to look at her, his eyes filled with fierce determination. "I'm not letting you go again."

Before she could respond, Corporal Thomas Humphery approached, his expression breaking for the moment. "Albert, Wales—what's the situation?"

Rebecca composed herself, slipping back into her role as Albert. "I made it to Jackson and Vicksburg," she said steadily. "The Confederates are holding strong in Vicksburg, but their resources are stretched thin. I saw civilians digging caves into the hillsides for shelter from the shelling."

Humphery nodded, his eyes widening with a mix of admiration and concern. "Vicksburg? You went there?"

"Yes," Rebecca—no, Albert—continued, her voice gaining a spark of energy. "I saw an ironclad slip past the Confederate guns. It was incredible, like nothing I have ever seen!"

Humphrey's face broke into a grin before his expression grew more thoughtful. "The caves are good to know about. We do not want to harm civilians if we can help it. I will let Aunt Todd know the shelling might get worse." He paused, assessing her. "How did you get out of Jackson?"

Rebecca's gaze flickered with the memory. "It was not easy. Daniel picked me up at the hotel where I was staying. We were being watched, even trailed. I had to slip into an alley and change clothes to blend in. But even that was not enough—I overheard soldiers planning to leave Jackson. Pemberton called all available troops to Vicksburg. They did not think there was any hope left for Jackson. Excellent work, Albert." He glanced around. "Where is Daniel?"

"He dropped me off," Rebecca replied, "said he was called somewhere else."

"Ahh… yes, very handy, our Daniel," said Thomas with a knowing nod.

Humphrey turned to leave, satisfied, but Wales was not done. As Rebecca followed, Wales caught her hand, his grip firm yet gentle, a contrast that startled her. She turned to look at him, surprise flickering in her eyes.

"Promise me you won't leave camp again," his voice soft and raw, his vulnerability caught her off guard.

Rebecca was at a loss for words, unused to seeing Wales—the stoic soldier, always composed—revealing such depth of emotion. For the first time, she felt the weight of his concern, his fear for her, and the unspoken connection between them. Her heart quickened as she realized how much he cared.

"I'll do my best, Wales," she whispered, her voice steady yet warm. In that moment, amidst the cold and chaos of war, she felt a rare sense of solace, of connection—of something she had not known she was missing.

With a final, lingering look, Wales released her hand, the tension in his eyes softening as he nodded. And though the battle raged on around them, for just that moment, they were two souls united against the storm.

*　　　*　　　*

Wales paced near the fire that night, watching the weary soldiers move about the camp as distant cannon fire rumbled through the evening air. His mind was not on the battle tonight—it was on Rebecca. Since her return, once again disguised as Albert Cashin, he could not shake the feeling that something was coming to a head. Tension among the men had become unbearable, and his own worry for her safety gnawed at him day and night.

A commotion close to the fire caught his attention. A gaunt, wild-eyed soldier from another regiment—Private Jacob Hensley of the 16th Iowa— had approached Rebecca, standing next to her, his posture threatening. Wales' heart pounded, and he moved near them, his eyes fixed on the two.

"Hey, you," Hensley barked, jabbing a finger toward Rebecca. "Where've you been, Cashin?"

Wales' jaw clenched, but he held back, watching Rebecca attempt to defuse the situation with a forced smile. This was not casual suspicion; this man was dangerous.

Rebecca's voice was steady, though Wales could hear the tension beneath. "I was out of town for a few days getting supplies, but I'm back now."

Hensley stepped in, his eyes narrowing. "Funny how the food tasted worse while you were gone. Now it is better again." He leaned in, his voice low and accusing. "Bet you're feeding information to the Rebs, aren't you?"

Rebecca's expression remained calm, but Wales saw a flicker of fear in her eyes. Just as Hensley's hand twitched toward his knife, Wales stepped forward, voice sharp and commanding.

"What's going on here?" His tone was calm but unyielding, his gaze fixed on Hensley.

Hensley spun around; face flushed with anger. "This one's a spy!" he spat and pointed at Rebecca. "Been sneaking around, feeding information to the Confederates!"

Wales' eyes flicked to Rebecca's pale face, then back to Hensley. "That's a serious accusation," he said, his voice cold as steel. "But you've got no proof."

"I do not need proof! Look at him—disappears for days, comes back, and nothing happens? I saw him! He is a traitor, and we all know it!"

Wales stepped closer, his presence forcing Hensley to back down. "We're all on edge," he said, his voice low. "But you're accusing one of us without a shred of evidence."

Hensley hesitated, glancing at the growing crowd of onlookers. He was losing ground, and he knew it. With a final glare at Rebecca, he muttered, "I'll be watching you, Cashin," before turning and stalking away.

As the other soldiers drifted back to their tasks, Wales exhaled, his shoulders relaxing as he turned to Rebecca. "You alright?" His voice softened now that the immediate threat was gone.

Rebecca nodded, though Wales could still see the tension in her body. "I am fine. Thank you," she said meeting his gaze.

He gave her a small smile, trying to ease the heaviness in his chest. "You managed that well. Just… be careful, all right? Fear and suspicion are spreading like wildfire around here."

"I will," Rebecca promised, but Wales could see the worry lingering in her eyes. He knew that Hensley's suspicion would not disappear easily.

That night, after the camp had settled into an uneasy quiet, Wales could not shake his lingering anxiety. As he lay in his tent, unable to sleep, he was jolted by a sudden cry.

"Samuel! Help!"

Wales bolted out of his tent, grabbing his rifle as he rushed to Rebecca's tent near the supply wagon. His heart pounded as he sprinted toward it, every worst-case scenario flashing through his mind. When he burst into the tent, the sight before him made his blood run cold.

Rebecca was backed into a corner, the wild-eyed Private Hensley stood before her with a knife raised, ready to strike. But before Wales could react, Samuel rushed in, tackling the attacker, and wrestling him to the ground.

"What the hell is wrong with you? You reek of gin!" Samuel shouted, his voice trembling with adrenaline as he pinned Hensley down.

Hensley screamed, thrashing beneath Samuel's grip. "He is a spy! I saw him sneaking off, meeting with the Confederates!"

Wales turned to Rebecca, her face pale, her breath coming in shallow gasps. He could see the fear in her eyes, the horror of being exposed, but she held herself silent, knowing her own words might deepen the suspicion festering in the camp.

Samuel glanced up at Rebecca, doubt clouding his face. "Albert… where did you go? Why won't you tell us?"

Wales' heart sank. The truth was closing in on her, and even Samuel—her closest ally in the camp—was beginning to falter.

Before Rebecca could respond, Thomas Humphery stormed into the tent, his expression livid. "What's going on here?" he demanded.

Samuel explained his hold on the now-subdued Hensley firm.

Humphrey's eyes were cold as he surveyed the scene. "Take this man back to his regiment and tell them to monitor him, or I will deal with him myself. Understood?"

Hensley, his drunken fury fading to exhaustion, offered no resistance as Samuel hauled him to his feet and escorted him out.

When they were alone, Wales turned to Rebecca, his heart breaking at the sight of her, still seated on the ground, trying to catch her breath. He knelt beside her, his voice low, urgent. "This can't go on, Rebecca."

Thomas nodded in agreement. "Wales is right. The longer you stay, the more they'll turn on you. You are not safe here. We will send you on another mission—this time to Vicksburg."

"No! That is not what I meant," Wales protested, his voice raw with emotion. "We need to send her back to New York!"

"We are in the middle of a siege, Wales. She would not make it back safely," Humphery replied, his tone pragmatic but firm.

Wales' face paled, his argument crumbling in the face of harsh reality. As much as he wanted to protect her, to keep her safe, he knew they could not guarantee her safety in New York any more than in the field.

He stared at her, his gaze filled with a mix of fear and longing. His hand brushed hers, a fleeting touch, but filled with meaning. "Promise me you'll be careful," his voice barely audible but she heard his words.

*   *   *

As darkness settled over the battlefield, Wales stood near the edge of camp, watching the horizon. The temporary truce Pemberton had brokered with Grant allowed an eerie silence to blanket the land from 2 p.m. to 8 p.m. Cannons had fallen silent, and soldiers from both sides—Union and Confederate— had ventured out to bury their dead. Across the trenches, enemies met not with weapons but with quiet reverence, each man honoring the fallen. There was no hatred in their gazes, only exhaustion and sorrow.

But for Wales, the truce meant something else. It was the chance he and Rebecca had been waiting for. He glanced at her, taking in the rare sight of her in civilian clothing—a simple, dark dress that softened her usual edges. Her hair, usually hidden beneath Albert's cap, was pulled back, her face shadowed by the setting sun. The contrast stirred something deep in his chest. She looked vulnerable, yet resolute, her eyes focused and steady.

Tonight, she would cross the lines again, slipping deeper into Vicksburg. Wales had been through her missions before, the constant worry gnawing at him whenever she was gone, but it never got easier. If anything, it was harder now, the fear sharper, knowing what each mission could mean.

They walked together as close to the Confederate line as they dared, staying in the shadows cast by tents and trees, the murmurs of soldiers around them blending into the night. Wales stopped at a secluded spot, and they turned to face each other.

"This is as far as I can go," he whispered, his voice strained, almost pleading. He took her hand, his fingers tightening around hers, the weight of unspoken words heavy in the air.

"Be careful, Rebecca," he murmured, his voice thick with emotion. "Come back to me."

She nodded, her throat tight, her eyes reflecting the same mix of fear and resolve. Unable to find the words, she squeezed his hand one last time and turned, disappearing into the darkness, her figure swallowed by the ridge as she crossed over the line. Her destination was Vicksburg to learn what she could in town and be an asset to spies already there.

Wales watched her go, dread coiling in his stomach. He felt powerless, knowing he could not follow, couldn't protect her. But then, the brief peace shattered.

A thunderous roar exploded across the battlefield as Confederate guns resumed their relentless shelling. Fiery trails streaked the night sky, and the ground shook beneath his feet. Wales' heart seized as he watched the explosions ripple through the very path Rebecca had taken.

The first blast lifted him off his feet, slamming him into the dirt. His head thudded against the ground, and the world dulled to a low hum, his ears ringing violently. He lay there, dazed, as the night lit up with fresh explosions, the horizon illuminated by fire and chaos.

"Rebecca!" The cry tore from his throat, raw and desperate. He scrambled to his feet, his vision swimming, and staggered forward, driven by a single, all-consuming action: I must find her.

He stumbled across the uneven ground, each step feeling like wading through quicksand. The night was alive with explosions, the air thick with dust and debris, but Wales' focus was fixed on the ridge, where Rebecca had vanished.

Just as he reached the edge of camp, another blast erupted nearby, the shockwave slamming into him, hurling him backward. Dust and smoke choked the air, stinging his eyes and lungs as he struggled to rise again. "No, no, no!" he yelled, his voice breaking as he forced himself forward, his legs burning with effort. Rebecca was out there. She needed him. He could not lose her—not like this.

Before he could take another step, strong hands grabbed his shoulders, jerking him back. John

Scobell was there, his face grim and set as the artillery barrage continued to rain down.

"Wales! Are you all right?" John shouted, his voice barely cutting through the ringing in Wales' ears.

Wales' wild eyes searched the ridge where he'd last seen Rebecca. "Rebecca! She is over there! I must—" His voice cracked, his arm pointing frantically toward the blasted terrain.

John's grip on him tightened, his expression hard and unyielding. "Wales, listen to me! We must get out of here! We cannot help her if we're dead!" he bellowed, giving Wales a shake, desperate to snap him out of his panic.

Wales fought against him; his movements frenzied. "No! I must find her! She is out there!" His heart thundered, the need to reach her overtaking any sense of self-preservation.

But John's hold was like iron. "We must go! We cannot do anything if we're dead!" he repeated, his voice cutting through Wales' desperation.

Wales' resistance wavered, his strength draining, but his heart felt as if it were being ripped apart. With one last look at the ridge, he allowed John to drag him back, stumbling with each step, his eyes fixed on the fiery chaos that swallowed the horizon.

Tears blurred his vision, frustration and helplessness boiled within him as they retreated into the camp, John's arm still gripped his shoulder firmly. Every step away from the ridge felt like a betrayal, his body moved only because he had no choice.

Back in the shelter of the lines, Wales sank to his knees, his chest heaving as the weight of everything settled on him. He had failed Rebecca. He could not protect her. And it tore him apart.

*   *   *

As Wales stood among the ranks of the 95th Illinois on the outskirts of Vicksburg, the weight of the past days pressed heavily on him. The failed charge on May 19th haunted him—images of fallen comrades, the relentless echo of gunfire, and the brutal chaos etched into his mind. But more than anything, he worried for Rebecca. She had crossed into Confederate lines once more, risking everything on a mission that he could not control or influence.

Wales tried to focus on the tasks at hand—the battle, the orders, keeping his men alive—but in the quiet moments, his mind drifted back to her. Where was she now? Had she made it to Vicksburg? Was she safe, or caught in the merciless shelling that hammered both sides day and night? Every time he heard the thunder of cannons or the sharp crack of musket fire, his heart lurched.

Now, on May 22nd, he and the 95th were ordered to charge once more. Under Colonel Humphrey's leadership, the regiment prepared to push forward, knowing the risks. The tension in the air was palpable, the surrounding men bracing themselves for what they knew awaited them. But amidst the growing anticipation, Wales could not shake his unease. Rebecca's absence weighed on him like a stone in his chest.

As they advanced toward the ridge, pushing through a tangled landscape of cane brake and fallen timber, Wales' focus wavered. He kept glancing around, as if he might spot her somewhere in the chaos, fighting alongside them. The futility of it gnawed at him—being trapped here in the brutality of battle, powerless to help her as she faced unknown dangers alone.

The charge was merciless. They reached the ridge, and instantly, Confederate artillery opened fire. Cannonballs screamed through the air, musket shots rained down, and the earth trembled beneath their feet. Wales ducked low, his eyes on Colonel Humphrey, who pressed forward with relentless determination, undeterred by the deadly barrage.

But as they advanced, the casualties mounted. Captain Manzer, Captain Cornwell—both struck down. Soldiers fell all around him, tearing the regiment apart by the ferocity of the Confederate defense. Then, in a single, terrifying instant, Colonel Humphrey disappeared. The ground where he had been standing erupted in a cloud of smoke and dirt, shrouding the area in confusion.

"Colonel Humphrey's fallen!" someone shouted, and Wales felt his stomach drop. The men faltered, hesitating as uncertainty rippled through the ranks. Some pressed forward in defiance, while others instinctively pulled back, the line breaking under the weight of loss and fear. For Wales, the sight of Humphrey going down was a bitter reminder of the merciless nature of war. If Humphrey—courageous, skilled, and unwavering—could fall, what chance did the rest of them have?

The order to withdraw was given, and Wales moved with the others, retreating to the comparative safety of a ravine. His body was battered, his muscles aching from the brutal advance, but his mind was elsewhere, gripped by a sharper pain. Rebecca had been gone too long. Since she had crossed that ridge, there had been no word, no sign of her. She was out there, surrounded by enemy forces, hurt or trapped, and he was powerless to reach her. The helplessness tore at him, clawing at his heart as they huddled in the ravine, regrouping after the crushing defeat.

As night fell, the remnants of the 95th gathered, exhaustion etched into their faces, the heavy silence underscoring their grief. The losses were staggering, and with Colonel Humphrey presumed dead, the morale of the regiment had plunged. The men murmured their fears among themselves; voices low.

"First Manzer, then Cornwell—and now Colonel Humphrey? How many more are we supposed to lose?" one soldier whispered, a hollow look in his eyes.

"It's like we're all marked," another replied, casting a glance toward the smoldering battlefield.

Wales sat among them, staring into the darkness, trying to ignore the nagging despair gnawing at him. The colonel's loss hung heavy over them all. Humphrey had been a symbol of strength, a figure that had kept them pressing forward even in the worst moments.

"Colonel Humphrey," a young private murmured, voice choked, "he would have wanted us to keep going. To see this through."

Someone muttered bitterly, "Easy to say when you are alive. This campaign's bleeding us dry."

Then, as if conjured by a rare stroke of fortune, Colonel Humphrey appeared in camp. Covered in dirt, his movements stiff, but very much alive. For a moment, the men stared, stunned into silence.

Then the silence broke.

"Colonel?" one soldier stammered; his voice tinged with disbelief. "It—it cannot be. We thought you were gone!"

A cheer went up, men surged forward, slapping Humphrey on the back, laughing and shouting in relief. "He is back! The Colonel's back!" The shock and joy rippled through the crowd, lifting the spirits of men who would all but given up hope.

But for Wales, the moment was bittersweet. He watched as the colonel shook hands and reassured his men, a faint smile on his own face as he tried to ease their concerns. For Wales, however, the sight of Humphrey's return was a grim reminder of how rare such miracles were. The colonel's survival was a miracle, but miracles were scarce in war. What about Rebecca?

One of the sergeants, still stunned, approached Humphrey. "Colonel, sir… we all thought you were gone. When we saw the blast—"

Humphrey brushed the dirt from his uniform, grimacing. "Thought I was gone myself. Took cover just in time." His voice was weary, but resolute. "We have lost too many good men today. I could not stand by and let you all think I'd left you."

The men nodded; admiration mixed with relief.

Humphrey met Wales' gaze, sensing the inner conflict there. "Lieutenant Wood, I need you focused. This siege will not get easier."

Wales nodded, swallowing the surge of emotion. "Yes, sir. I am… glad you're back."

Humphrey clasped him on the shoulder, understanding the deeper sentiment in Wales' eyes. "Keep faith, Wood. Sometimes we get through by a hair's breadth, but we get through." He gave Wales a knowing look, a silent acknowledgment of the unspoken burdens Wales carried.

As the men dug in for the siege that Grant had ordered, Wales stared out toward the enemy lines, his heart heavy with dread. The battle for Vicksburg was far from over, and neither was his waiting. Every roar of artillery, every burst of musket fire, held a new weight, each one a reminder of how close death lingered.

He clenched his jaw, forcing himself to hope that somewhere out there, Rebecca was finding her own way through the storm.

Chapter Eleven

Rebecca lay motionless, half-buried under dirt and debris that had cascaded down the ravine. A high-pitched ringing filled her ears, drowning out every other sound, and her right arm throbbed with a sharp, searing pain that made her vision blur. She struggled to draw breath, her mind hazy and disoriented from the blast.

Gritting her teeth, she tried to piece together her surroundings, but before she could gather her strength to move, she heard voices—Confederate soldiers speaking with a southern drawl, close by. Her heart pounded as she strained to listen, every muscle tensing.

"I swear, I saw someone come this way!" one soldier muttered, his voice laced with suspicion.

Rebecca's breath stilled. She pressed herself deeper into the dirt, her body blending into the debris as best she could. She could hear the crunch of boots on loose earth, the footsteps inching closer, her pulse racing with each step.

"Probably just the smoke messing with your eyes," another soldier grumbled, though his voice held a note of doubt. "Ain't nobody here."

Rebecca held her breath, muscles aching from the effort to stay still, wishing herself to be invisible. The footsteps lingered, shuffling around, and she imagined their eyes sweeping over the landscape, scanning every inch for signs of movement.

Then, after a tense pause, she heard them move away, their footsteps growing fainter until they vanished altogether. She waited moments longer, making sure they were gone, before exhaling a shaky breath.

Her body trembled as she gathered her strength, forcing herself to crawl in the opposite direction, moving inch by agonizing inch. Each jolt of movement sent a wave of pain through her arm, but she pushed it to the back of her mind, focusing instead on getting away from the battlefield. Vicksburg was her hope of shelter, but it felt like an impossible distance as she dragged herself over the uneven terrain, her vision swimming with each effort.

Suddenly, the familiar, shrill whistle of an incoming shell pierced the air, its tone cutting through the chaotic sounds of battle. Rebecca's heart skipped as she tried to crawl out of its path. But she had no time—the shell landed close, the force of the explosion rocking the ground beneath her and sending a brutal shockwave through her body.

The blast hurled her to the side, dust and debris filled her lungs and stung her eyes. She landed hard, her body half-numb from the impact, but she forced herself to keep moving, desperate to get away before anyone spotted her or another shell hit close by.

Each movement was a struggle, the pain in her arm intensifying with every inch she gained. She bit back a cry, her face coated with dirt and sweat, as she clawed her way forward. Above her, the shelling continued, each blast seeming closer than the last, the sky flashing in angry bursts of light.

Rebecca fought to stay conscious. Her mind narrowed to a single goal: survive.

*   *   *

Rebecca's body felt heavy and unresponsive, though her mind swirled in a fog of pain and confusion. The darkness enveloped her, but through the haze, she felt a faint shuffle of feet nearby. Her instincts told her to stay still, to avoid detection, but the pain in her arm throbbed with every beat of her heart.

Then she knew it—a hand on her head, brushing away the dirt and debris. A voice, distant but clear, broke through the silence. "She is alive! How did she get out of here?"

Another voice responded, "Must have been scouting for food, unfortunate thing. Got caught when they started shelling."

Rebecca tried to open her eyes, but they remained shut, her body refusing. She was lifted, strong arms cradling her as if she were weightless. The motion was careful, but each step sent jolts of pain through her, making her want to cry out, though no sound escaped her lips.

She floated as if carried and then placed on a wagon. The rough wooden planks jostled beneath her, each bump and creak a reminder of her fragile state. The ringing in her ears had lessened, replaced by the steady rumble of the wagon wheels and the muted murmur of voices.

Then, through the din, she heard a voice—familiar, urgent, filled with concern. "Alice! It is Alice! I know her!"

Rebecca's mind struggled to place the voice, but it was as if her thoughts submerged in deep water.

The voice grew closer, more distinct, and then she felt a soft hand on her cheek.

"Oh, Dr. Flanders, take her to my cave," the voice pleaded.

Rebecca's heart fluttered as the name came to her: Mary Webster Loughborough. She wanted to speak, to let Mary know she was aware, but her body betrayed her, remaining still and silent as the wagon continued its journey. The solace she found, she knew she was no longer alone.

*   *   *

Rebecca awoke to a dim, flickering light casting shadows across the rough-hewn walls of a spacious cave. The air was cool and damp, though the oppressive humidity of the Mississippi outdoors seemed to seep in at the edges, a reminder of the world waiting beyond these walls. She lay on a makeshift bed—a simple cot padded with blankets that rested on the dirt floor, carrying a faint, earthy scent of musty soil.

The cave, though spacious, had a low ceiling with shovel marks etched into the packed dirt, a testament to its hurried construction. Along one wall, a small bookshelf brought from a nearby home held various supplies—candles, medicines, and an assortment of non-perishable foods. Rebecca's stomach tightened, and she made a mental note to see what sort of food she could find there.

Near the cave's entrance was a small table and a couple of chairs, set up to serve as a dining or meeting area. Seated there was Mary Loughborough, speaking in hushed tones to a young Black man who looked to be about sixteen or seventeen. Rebecca guessed he was a servant—or more accurately, a slave—risking a great deal to be here with them.

"Ma'am! She is awake!" he said as his eyes landed on Rebecca.

"Shh… George, not so loud," Mary murmured, glancing over at Rebecca with a gentle smile.

"Yes, Ma'am," George replied, though his eyes sparkled with relief. "Do you need anything else besides the vegetables your husband sent? Does not look like the shelling's stopping soon. Best you stay here."

"Thank you, George. We are grateful—it was a significant risk bringing those here," Mary's voice soft but warm as she watched him settle by the fire near the entrance.

Rebecca's gaze drifted further around the cave, taking in the refuge Mary had made from these stark surroundings. Rugs and blankets spread across the floor to ward off the chill of the ground, while personal items—books, small family heirlooms, and delicate, well-worn trinkets—arranged to add touches of comfort. Beyond the canvas door that covered the cave's entrance, a small fire crackled, filling the air with a gentle warmth and the earthy scent of burning wood.

Despite the cave's humble setup, a feeling of security settled over Rebecca. The thick, dirt walls shielded them from the chaos outside, muffling the echoes of distant shelling and the tension of the war. Mary had done her best to recreate a sense of normalcy here, and it showed in the careful details and calm she projected, even in these trying circumstances.

Rebecca's eyes adjusted to the dim light, and her mind cleared from the haze of unconsciousness. She felt a warmth in her chest—a small measure of safety and gratitude for the care surrounding her here in this unexpected sanctuary.

In the dim, flickering light of Mary Loughborough's cave, Rebecca lay still, letting the quiet murmurs of Mary and George drift around her like a soothing balm. The ache in her bruised limbs reminded her of the close calls she had survived, but here, beneath the thick earth walls, she was safe—at least for the moment. Yet, despite the safety of the cave, her mind churned with worry, caught between recovery and a gnawing urgency to complete her mission.

Rebecca shifted, suppressing a grimace as the shelling outside continued, a constant, distant rumble that shook the cave and made her restless. She had learned the rhythm of the bombardment, a routine that had become second nature to the people of Vicksburg. Mary explained the "schedule" of the shelling as if it were a grim daily chore.

"At four in the morning, the shrapnel is thrown more furiously than at any other time," Mary had recounted. "Around seven, the Minie balls start falling, joined by Parrott shells, canisters, solid shot—everything they can throw at us. Every minute of the day, there's a constant artillery barrage from the Union lines."

Rebecca could not help but marvel at Mary's calmness. "So constant were the projectiles," Mary added, "that I almost grew indifferent to them myself."

Rebecca listened as Mary described the lives of those around them who had adapted to this underground existence. Entire families had fled to the bluffs, transforming caves into makeshift homes. The demand for caves had grown so high that it had become a booming business; those who could afford it paid handsomely for larger, more comfortable spaces. Some of these caves had rooms, timber braces, and even multiple chambers.

Mary's cave, ordered by her husband before she arrived, was simple but sturdily built. About six feet deep, it allowed Mary to stand upright, a rare luxury in the dug refuges around Vicksburg. She spoke of the cave diggers who had set their prices according to the demand: twenty dollars for a single-room cave, fifty dollars for those with extra chambers—a price many were willing to pay for security.

Rebecca marveled at the stories Mary shared. One evening, Mary had taken shelter with sixty-five others crammed into a single cave room, "packed like sardines in a box," she had said, with a sideways smile. On another night, over two hundred people had crowded together during a heavy bombardment, each one huddling against the dirt walls, seeking comfort in numbers.

Despite the unending danger, a strange routine had settled into this life underground. People ventured out during lulls in the shelling to gather supplies or salvage what they could from their battered homes, careful not to stray far from their shelters. The bluffs offered some protection from the Federal artillery, but safety was relative here.

Rebecca, amazed at the resilience of the people around her even as she gathered information, became aware of the crucial details she would need to relay to Wales and Thomas. Vicksburg was stretched thin; food was scarce, and morale was fading. These insights, though grim, were valuable, yet for now, she stayed quiet, observing and blending in.

One evening, as they sat around a small fire that filled the cave with a soft warmth and the faint aroma of the thin stew they were cooking, Rebecca subtly turned the conversation. "Mary," she began, stirring the pot, "you mentioned your husband is with the Confederate forces. How do the people here feel about what is happening?"

Mary silenced, her hands pausing as she chopped the last of the vegetables they had. Her gaze grew distant for a moment before she spoke. "It is mixed, honestly. Some still support the cause with every fiber, but others... they are worn down, only tired of it all. Supplies are low, and with the Union forces so close, there is a constant tension."

Rebecca nodded, absorbing the information, confirming what she had suspected. Vicksburg was on the brink, its people struggling, its morale frayed. She kept her reaction neutral, responding, "It's understandable, given how long this siege has dragged on."

"Yes," Mary sighed, wiping her hands. "It is hard on everyone. We are all just trying to survive, day by day. But…" She gave a faint, sad smile, her gaze softening. "We do what we must."

Rebecca nodded, returning Mary's smile, grateful for the woman's openness, though her mind remained sharp, processing every word.

*   *   *

The heat of the day had simmered down, leaving a hint of coolness in the air that made starting the cook fire almost bearable. Rebecca glanced up as a low rumble echoed from the horizon. It was not thunder—it was the distant roar of Union artillery, hammering Vicksburg with relentless intensity.

With George's help, the fire sparked to life, casting flickering shadows on the rough cave walls. Rebecca watched as George sliced the mule meat into portions, her mind working on how to stretch their meager supplies. Every meal was a challenge, each ration a gamble in how long they could make their food last.

"George, we're going to jerk a portion of this meat," she instructed, raising her voice to be heard over the faint, steady drum of artillery. "We will dry it out. Dig a small cave off the ridge and rig up sticks to hang the strips. Keep a slow fire beneath it—it will dry the meat enough to preserve it. We need this to last as long as possible."

George gave her a tense, approving nod, a hint of admiration in his eyes as he looked back to the task. "Ma'am, I am amazed at what you can think up," he said, his voice laced with a mixture of awe and fear as another shell burst somewhere outside, sending a faint shudder through the ground beneath them.

"Hunger makes a person resourceful," Rebecca murmured, placing a pan over the fire to cook the remaining portion of the meat. The muted explosion of a distant shell punctuated the soft sizzle of meat, and she paused, gripping the pan's handle as she listened. She wondered how much longer they could last through this siege. How much closer would the shelling get before even this shelter would no longer be safe?

For weeks, mule meat had become their staple, though its taste and texture were barely tolerable. Mary had shared stories of desperate measures taken before the siege: citizens trying to stockpile whatever they could, only to find it was not enough. Mary herself had survived mostly on rice and milk, boiling the rice, and eating it cold, barely able to summon the will to eat. "I've grown indifferent to hunger," Mary had admitted, her voice cracking. Rebecca understood that feeling now, too; even this pitiful meal might be the last decent one for days.

George's daily ventures into town were a lifeline, each trip fraught with risk, each return a small victory. Every time he left, Rebecca's heart held tight until he returned, fearing he might not make it back. When he arrived that night, his expression was grim as he set down a bundle of scarce provisions—rice, a handful of dried beans, and a small bag of salt.

Rebecca stared at the meager supplies, her mind drifting to the soaring prices she'd heard about - two hundred dollars for a barrel of flour, a hundred for a bushel of corn, five dollars a pound for bacon— if it could even be found. Desperation was visible everywhere in Vicksburg: smuggled goods sold at outrageous prices, families forced to barter and scrape by on whatever they could find.

As George worked, his gaze lingered on the knife in Rebecca's hand. His expression grew serious, and his voice dropped to a whisper that rose above the sound of distant explosions. "There's something strange about that knife."

Rebecca stilled, her fingers tightening around the handle. "What do you mean?" she whispered, her eyes flicking toward the cave's entrance, half-expecting a shell to burst through the thin barrier at any moment.

George leaned closer; his face taut with caution. "Look closely… and be careful." Straightening, he moved away, turning to address Mary, who was organizing the few remaining supplies. "Mrs. Mary, I stopped by your husband's company on my way back," he said, diverting any suspicion from Rebecca.

Rebecca looked down at the knife, her pulse quickening. It appeared ordinary—old and worn—but George's words had set off a quiet alarm. She inspected the handle, and after a moment, she noticed a small gap at the end, barely visible. Was it a simple flaw, or something more?

With her heart pounding, she grabbed a spoon and wedged its edge into the gap. She felt a faint click, and to her surprise, a tiny, rolled piece of paper slipped out of the handle. Her breath caught as she unrolled it, her eyes scanning the brief, cryptic message: "We know. Send out. Hospital. June 20."

Rebecca's mind raced, her mind a tangle of questions. Who was "we"? What did they know? And what was set to happen at the hospital on June 20? She folded the note and tucked it into her pocket, casting a quick, grateful glance toward George, who gave her the faintest nod in acknowledgment.

Rebecca stirred the cooking mule meat, her gaze unfocused, her mind turning over the mysterious message and its implications. Each piece of information felt like a fragment of a larger, dangerous puzzle, one that was closing in on her. She felt the weight of the secret now hidden in her pocket, her senses sharper, her heart more wary. The note in the knife's handle deepened her unease.

As the fire crackled and the faint scent of cooking meat filled the air, Rebecca steeled herself. Every action, every whispered exchange, was fraught with risk. Yet, in this cave surrounded by the siege's constant threat, she knew she had to keep going.

*　　*　　*

In the pitch-black cover of night, the moon shone bright enough to light Rebecca's path, making a candle unnecessary as she descended the hillside toward the city hospital like the note said. She moved down the narrow trail that wove through dense undergrowth before slipping onto Main Street and ducking into an alley.

Every sound heightened her senses, her pulse thrumming as she approached the hospital. Her hand reached for the knife in her pocket. For a tense second, she weighed her options—fight or flee—but the figure veered left into another alley. Rebecca exhaled, relieved but rattled, and continued toward her destination.

But before she could regain her composure, the night exploded into chaos the moment after she reached the hospital.

A massive shell, at least fifteen inches in diameter, screamed overhead from the river, launched by a Union gunboat. The sound was piercing, otherworldly, as it arced through the sky and struck the upper floors of the hospital. A blinding flash lit up the street, followed by a deafening boom.

Rebecca threw herself to the ground, covering her head as debris rained down, bricks and mortar slamming into the road where she had been standing seconds before. The force of the explosion rocked the ground, and she scrambled to her feet, darting for cover behind a pile of rubble just as another shell screamed through the air.

The second explosion shook the entire block. Rebecca's ears rang as the blast sent chunks of brick and plaster hurtling down. She sprinted toward the hospital entrance, her legs burning as she pushed herself forward. The doors blown inward, leaving the entrance exposed, and inside, chaos reigned.

The shell had torn through one of the upper floors, sending shockwaves throughout the building. Rebecca ducked as more debris tumbled from above, avoiding a beam that crashed to the floor beside her. Screams echoed down the hallways, a harrowing blend of fear and pain that mingled with the relentless ringing in her ears. Wounded soldiers crawled or dragged to safety, their blood smearing across the dust-caked floor as smoke filled the air.

Another explosion rocked the hospital. Shrapnel whizzed through the corridor, slicing through anything in its path. Rebecca dove behind the reception desk as a chunk of metal embedded itself in the wall beside her. She stole a glance over her shoulder, horror twisting her stomach as she saw a wall collapse onto three men who had been dragging themselves toward safety. The impact was immediate and devastating, burying them under tons of rubble.

The aftermath was gruesome. She saw eight people lying dead around her, their lives extinguished in an instant, and a nurse told her of fourteen others seriously wounded. The hospital, already at its breaking point, was barely holding together. The stench of blood and smoke choked the air as nurses tended to the injured, pulling them away from danger and into whatever shelter the battered hospital could still offer.

Rebecca surveyed the scene, her mind racing. She was not supposed to be here, but the chaos might give her the perfect chance to slip away unnoticed. She glanced around, seeing the nurses and soldiers too overwhelmed by the carnage to notice her. She seized her opportunity.

Keeping low, she darted down a side hallway, avoiding the main paths where she might be spotted. The floor was slick with blood, and she nearly slipped, catching herself against the wall as she fought to stay on her feet. The thunder of her breath filled her ears as she reached a back walkway veiled by shadows.

The bombardment showed no sign of stopping. As Rebecca fled down the deserted street, another shell exploded nearby, hurling her to the ground. The shockwave knocked the air from her lungs, and for a terrifying moment, she could not breathe. She gasped, her vision swimming, but forced herself upright, stumbling into an alley.

Her heart pounded as she ducked behind a crumbling wall, steadying her breath and quieting her mind. That is when she heard a voice—a sudden whisper in the darkness.

"Miss, my Aunt Todd sent me to see you."

Rebecca whipped around, but she froze when a dust-covered young boy stepped forward from the shadows, his wide eyes catching the faint flicker of distant fires. Recognizing the code phrase, she relaxed—this was her contact.

"Yes, good to know," she replied in a faint voice, pocketing her pistol.

Reaching into her pocket, she pulled out a small spool of thread, innocuous but hiding a rolled note inside the barrel. It contained crucial information she had gathered: enemy positions, weaknesses, and the Union's next moves. She handed it to the boy, her eyes scanning the street for danger.

"Get this to them quickly," Rebecca instructed, her tone calm but firm. "And be careful."

The boy nodded, pocketing the spool with practiced ease.

Chapter Twelve

As Confederate artillery intensified, the men of the 95th Illinois pushed forward under Wales's direction, each step fraught with peril as shells exploded around them, scattering dirt, rock, and smoke into the air. The sound was deafening, a relentless barrage that shook the earth beneath their feet, but Wales's voice cut through the chaos as he barked commands, rallying his men.

Amidst the turmoil, Corporal Thomas Humphery rushed up beside him, his face streaked with sweat and grime, his rifle gripped tightly. "Captain! Samuel Pepper's squad took a hit from the last barrage—they are pinned down, but he is pulling the men together!"

Wales's gaze shifted down the line, spotting Samuel Pepper, bloodied but unyielding as he worked to rally his battered squad. "We will cover them, Thomas. Get to his position—tell him we are advancing on my mark."

Thomas gave a quick nod and sprinted off, weaving through the smoke and debris. Wales turned to his own squad, his voice fierce and resolute. "We need to move! They have got men trapped ahead. Stay low and keep your eyes sharp! We push in five—watch for artillery fire!"

The men gave a brief, tense nod, bracing themselves as they huddled close to the ground. Together, Wales, Thomas, and Samuel's squads began a grueling crawl toward the next line of trenches, narrowly dodging incoming shells that sent shrapnel whistling through the air. Wales could feel the tremors from each explosion reverberate through his bones, the ground alive with shockwaves.

When they reached Samuel's position, another shell struck nearby, the impact sending a shower of debris over them. Thomas signaled to Pepper, who acknowledged with a quick, grim nod as he rallied his squad, his voice hoarse but steady.

"Good to see you both in one piece!" Samuel shouted over the thunderous noise, his eyes darting between the approaching Union line and the looming Confederate fortifications.

Wales placed a firm hand on his shoulder, the gesture a brief but solid reassurance. "Hold fast, Samuel. This line will not break. We are pushing through together."

Samuel gave a determined nod, and Wales turned to address the assembled men, his voice rising above the clamor of the battlefield. "Today, we break through! Together, we hold the line and take the fight to them. Move forward—no one gets left behind!"

As the signal for the assault echoed down the line, Wales, Samuel, and Thomas led the charge. The men surged forward, their voices drowned out by the relentless roar of artillery, but their focus unyielding. The ground shook beneath their feet with each pounding shell, but they pressed onward, advancing toward the Confederate lines with grit and unwavering resolve.

In that brutal moment, amidst the smoke and thunder, Wales knew they were fighting not just for the battle but for each other. With Samuel and Thomas by his side, he led his men forward, determined to carve a path through the chaos and break the enemy's hold.

*   *   *

The siege of Vicksburg wore on, progressing at a slow, grinding pace that tested every ounce of patience and resilience among the men. Over the past ten days, the 95th Illinois had intensified its efforts, digging deeper rifle pits, erecting new batteries, and inching their lines ever closer to the entrenched enemy. Secret mines were being carved beneath the earth, packed with explosives designed to shatter Confederate defenses at Fort Hill, on the Jackson Road—their perceived gateway to seizing Vicksburg itself.

The strain of the siege, etched into every thread of their uniforms. Once-proud blue coats, issued with ceremony and pride by the Union, were now little more than rags, held together by sewn patches and threadbare seams. The relentless southern sun added to their hardship, its heat forcing the men to restrict movement during the peak hours to conserve strength and sanity alike.

With July approaching, Wales's mind drifted to the Fourth—a day of celebration that had once marked with laughter, speeches, and parades. This year, he hoped they would mark the day within Vicksburg's walls, celebrating their independence but a hard-won victory if the mines and their ongoing push broke through Confederate defenses.

On June 5th, the air in camp lightened as the men gathered around the long-awaited supply wagons. Wales stood with Corporal Thomas Humphery and John Scobell, watching Samuel Pepper hurry over, his face a mix of relief and excitement.

"Finally, some good news!" Samuel said with a grin, clapping Thomas on the back. "Feels like Christmas morning, doesn't it?"

Thomas laughed; his eyes bright as he scanned the crates of supplies. "It sure does, though I reckon Santa wouldn't fancy dodging cannon fire on his rounds."

John, always the quiet realist, nodded toward the wagons. "Here is hoping it is more than just socks and salt pork. A bit of fresh powder and shot would brighten my day."

As they unpacked, distributing new uniforms and food among the men, Wales could not help but notice how even these simple necessities felt like luxuries. But the sight of clean uniforms, if only briefly, brought a renewed sense of dignity and purpose to his weary regiment.

The following day, June 6th, brought them back to the grim realities of war. Ducking and dodging bullets, Wales spoke to his men, his tone firm as gunfire cracked in the distance. "Stay low and move fast. Every shadow could be a shelter, and every sound could be your last warning." His gaze moved down the line, reinforcing the weight of his words.

June 7th saw them taking a ruthless edge as they devised a sharpshooting ruse. Wales watched as an effigy carefully positioned to draw enemy fire. He called out to his sharpshooters, "Ready? Let them think they have caught us off guard." The strategy worked as intended, and a barrage of fire came from the enemy lines.

Lying prone beside him, Thomas smirked, his voice low and amused. "Your trick's paying dividends, Captain."

Wales peered through his binoculars, a faint smile on his face as he watched the enemy's confusion. "Every mistake they make is an opportunity for us," he replied, his voice grim but satisfied.

On June 8th, a new idea emerged as they used cotton bales for makeshift cover, water-soaked to resist enemy fire. Wales and John supervised as the bales strategically positioned.

"It's crude, but it's clever," Wales remarked, approving of the ingenuity. "Let's see how they like a taste of their own fire."

John nodded, aligning one of the bales. "Using the noggin. But let us not get cocky—they are bound to catch on eventually."

By June 10th, as they fortified their makeshift quarters, Samuel brought humor into the day's drudgery, remarking, "I never thought I'd be a part-time carpenter in the army, Captain."

Wales chuckled, wiping the sweat from his brow. "Every skill's a step toward survival, Pepper. Keep at it."

The levity was short-lived. On June 11th, a mortar shell struck near Wales's tent, the impact shaking the ground and leaving a haze of dust and smoke. Shaken but unharmed, he rallied his men. "Stay sharp, lads! They are not letting up, and neither will we!"

Thomas, inspecting the area, muttered grimly, "Too close for comfort, Wales. We need to rethink our placements."

Wales nodded; his expression resolute. "We will reassess at sundown. For now, stay vigilant—no mistakes."

June 12th brought a more reflective moment as they discussed pay. After dinner, sitting together on overturned crates, John mused aloud, "Money is no good to the dead. Let us make sure we put it to wise use, eh?"

Wales glanced around at his men, his heart swelling with a mix of pride and concern. "Every dollar we send home is a promise that we are coming back. Let us make sure we keep that promise."

These exchanges—each day's dialogue, from planning tactical ruses to sharing jokes—buoyed their spirits, reinforcing the bonds that kept them going. Every command, every laugh, every knowing glance between them underscored the strength of their camaraderie, as they faced the relentless siege together with unyielding resolve.

*   *   *

Wales clenched his fists, his gaze fixed on the distant glow of shellfire over Vicksburg. Each explosion sent a shudder through him, a brutal reminder that Rebecca was down there, caught in that living nightmare. It was his fault she was there, trapped in this siege. She could have been anywhere else, living a life untouched by the constant threat of death, but she had chosen this path. And he had been the one to draw her into it. The weight of guilt gnawed at him, each burst of fire and smoke over the city sinking that guilt deeper.

He remembered the day he had first seen her disguised as Albert Cashin—fearless, focused, a fierce glint in her eyes. He could still remember the shock of realizing who she was, the complexity of her bravery hidden behind a mask. If he had foreseen what this mission would lead her to, would he have acted differently? Part of him knew he would have tried to stop her, tried to keep her away from this danger. But he also knew that nothing would have dissuaded her once she had committed herself to the cause. Rebecca had a strength and resolve that matched, if not surpassed, his own. That was why he had dared to hope she could manage this, why he had trusted her to see it through.

But now, watching the relentless bombardment, he felt the cold hand of doubt. War was indiscriminate in its cruelty. No matter how brave or skilled a person was, all it took was one shell, one bullet, to strip everything away. The thought twisted painfully in his chest. She was down there, somewhere under those blazing skies, sheltering in caves, dodging fire, and destruction. How long could anyone endure that, much less a woman?

The sight of those shells raining down fueled something fierce within him—a resolve that burned against the darkness. He would make this right. Whatever it took, he would see her safe again, away from this hellish war. She deserved a life beyond hiding in caves and fleeing from artillery, a life with the freedom she had risked so much to secure. He would repay her courage and loyalty.

As he stood beneath the dark sky, the explosions lighting his face in brief, harsh flashes, Wales swore to himself: he would do whatever it took to make that future possible for her, Rebecca, his love.

*   *   *

The siege of Vicksburg wore on, each day blurring into the next with the endless rhythm of cannon fire and the grueling labor of trench work. From his vantage point, Captain Wales Wood watched the grim tableau unfold: Union artillery thundered across the landscape, a reminder of their power and resources, while Vicksburg suffered under the relentless assault. Every shell, every explosion, sent a pang of worry through him, knowing that Rebecca was down there, enduring the very heart of the chaos.

Though the Union soldiers were well-supplied, each meal a reassuring sign of the upper hand they held, Wales heard a different story from the Confederate prisoners they occasionally captured. Listening to these men, he understood the desperation within the city's walls—a desperation so deep that the contrast between the two sides felt surreal. While Union soldiers still had ample food, fresh water, and rations delivered regularly, the Confederate soldiers they encountered painted a bleaker picture.

One prisoner, an older Confederate with a worn face and hollow eyes, confessed, "We are down to eating mule, Captain. Most of the cornmeal's gone, too. What is left barely qualifies as food."

Another soldier, hardly more than a boy, nodded grimly. "Rats, too, if you're lucky enough to catch one," he said, his voice hollow. The young soldier's eyes told a story of hunger and desperation beyond anything words could capture.

Wales listened in silence, a reluctant pity stirring within him. The war had twisted everything familiar, pushing men and boys alike to the edge of human endurance. The contrast struck him sharply—while Union soldiers dined on hardtack, bacon, and coffee, their enemies were scraping for scraps and setting traps for rats, hoping for a meager meal. Even the most fastidious tastes reduced to survival by any means, a bitter reminder that war spared no one.

The stories of desperation grew as the siege dragged into July, the oppressive heat making each day feel longer than the last. More Confederate prisoners confirmed the hunger gnawing away at them, their once-proud defenses weakened by the simple, unrelenting force of starvation. When they spoke, Wales saw the strain etched into their faces, heard it in their voices. Even the strongest patriotism couldn't quell the emptiness that ate away at them from within.

Chapter Thirteen

Rebecca returned to the cave where Mary and George had made their makeshift home, her steps heavy from the grim events of the night. Outside, the relentless shelling around Vicksburg created a steady rumble, a chilling backdrop to their confinement. Inside, the dim light of a small fire cast flickering shadows along the earthen walls, deepening the closeness of the space.

The hills surrounding Vicksburg dotted with caves, yet these shelters revealed the stark social divides even in wartime. Rebecca had seen the spacious, furnished caves of the wealthier families—where the war seemed an inconvenience, not a dire threat. She imagined her own family doing the same as if they were here: sitting around oil lamps, murmuring over tea, trying to keep a fragile veneer of normalcy as the world outside fell apart. *Someday I will be able to tell them about all of this.*

Mary's cave, though more modest, lay in an upper-class section, offering slightly more privacy than the cramped, shared shelters where families huddled together in fear. The sorrowful cries and anxious murmurs drifting from those crowded caves wove themselves into the night's symphony of artillery fire, each new shell igniting cries that pierced Rebecca's heart. She knew these experiences would haunt her forever.

"Oh, Alice! Where did you go?" Mary's voice broke through, and Rebecca managed to put on a small smile. "I needed…a walk to clear my head. The bombing is unnerving." Mary was already talking a mile a minute, her words light but tinged with exhaustion. "Oh yes, it is! Don't worry, we are safe here! I have just been telling George all about my James, and I don't think he minds listening. He is a good soul, our George." She sighed, staring dreamily at the cave entrance as if her husband might walk through it at any moment. "James always insisted I stay close. 'If you're near,' he would say, 'I know you are safe. I can look out for you.' And I feel that way even now. Just knowing he is somewhere in this city keeps me steady."

Rebecca offered a sympathetic nod. Mary's love for James seemed to insulate her from the fear that gripped everyone else. She clung to each memory of him as if it were armor against the chaos.

Mary went on, her tone lightening. "I will tell you, Alice, the things I brought! You'd think I was setting up a summer house—bonnets, silk gloves, my favorite China set! I even packed a feathered fan," she laughed, a sound that was out of place in their bleak surroundings. "When we first moved here, James just smiled and let me fuss over setting everything up. 'Bring what you like,' he said. 'If it makes you happy, then it makes me happy.'"

As Mary continued her story, George moved about the cave with quiet purpose, starting a small fire for cooking. He glanced at Mary now and then, steady patience in his gaze as he listened to her endless stream of anecdotes.

Suddenly, Mary's eyes lit up with excitement. "Oh, Alice, did I tell you about the night he proposed? It was at a grand ball in New York. He dropped to one knee right there on the dance floor—no ring, mind you, but he said he just could not wait!" She sighed, her gaze softening at the memory. "We danced all night after that, laughing like fools. 'I'll get you a ring soon enough,' he promised. 'But I had to let you know you're mine.'"

Rebecca smiled at the story, distracted from the dangers outside. Mary's voice, filled with memories of better times, made the cold cave feel almost warm.

But suddenly, a high-pitched whistle sliced through the air, shattering their small moment of comfort. Rebecca barely had time to react before a shell tumbled into the cave entrance, skidding to a stop just feet away.

"Lord have mercy!" Mary gasped, her face going pale as she froze in terror.

Rebecca acted on instinct, pulling Mary close. "Stay down!" she commanded, her heart racing.

But George was already in motion. Without a word, he sprang to his feet, his eyes locked on the shell. "I got it!" he shouted, rushing toward the deadly object.

"No, George, don't!" Rebecca cried, her hand reaching out in desperation. But George did not hesitate. He bent down, scooped up the shell with both hands, and sprinted toward the entrance.

"George, no!" Mary's voice broke with fear, her hand clutching tightly to Rebecca's arm.

In a swift, powerful motion, George hurled the shell as far as he could beyond the mouth of the cave. A heartbeat of dread followed, then a thunderous explosion just outside. Dust and small rocks rained down, coating everything in a fine layer of dirt as the force of the blast rippled through the cave.

When the dust settled, George stood at the entrance, coughing but unharmed. He turned back to them with a calm grin, though his hands trembled. "Ain't nothin' to be 'afeared of now, Mrs. Mary and Miss Alice," he said in his usual steady voice.

Mary's eyes filled with tears, her voice a soft whisper. "George… you could've been killed."

Rebecca felt a swell of admiration and relief as she brushed dirt from her skirt. She stepped forward, placing a hand on his shoulder. "George, that was… I have never seen courage like that. Thank you."

George nodded, his usual calmness returning. "Jus' doin' what I promised, Miss."

As they sat down to catch their breath, Rebecca glanced at George, remembering his keen awareness—the way he had looked at the knife handle days earlier. A knowing gleam in his eyes.

That night when Mary dozed off, George leaned over to Rebecca, his voice low. "Reckon that knife of yours has more than just steel in it, don't it, miss?"

Rebecca was tense, though she tried to keep her expression neutral. "What makes you say that, George?"

He gave her a faint smile. "I have had to keep my eyes open, Miss. Learned to see things others miss. I saw you studying that knife, looking it over carefully. I know a secret when I see one." His voice softened, his gaze steady. "And I saw through your story the moment you walked in. Ain't never met a Confederate widow as sharp as you."

Rebecca's heart pounded, though George's calm demeanor reassured her. "How long have you known?"

"Since the start," he said, his eyes filled with quiet understanding. "I knew you were not here just to 'find kinfolk.' Knew you were here for something bigger. And do not worry, Miss—I ain't tellin' no one. Just think of me when those Union troop's ride into town, ok?"

She felt a wave of gratitude, a feeling she rarely experienced in her line of work. George was a rare ally—someone who saw her truth and protected it. She nodded, her voice soft. "I will. Thank you, George. For everything."

George settled back; his face illuminated by the dim light of the fire. "Jus' doin' what I promised, Miss," he repeated, a steady reassurance in his tone.

Mary stirred awake then, her voice breaking the quiet. "George has been my faithful defender through every hardship. When this is over, I will do all I can to make sure he's free."

Rebecca's gaze met George's. "I'll help too, Mary," she said, her voice firm. "He deserves it more than anyone."

Rebecca, seeking a distraction from the relentless bombardment and gnawing hunger, engaged George in conversation during one of the worst spells of shelling. They huddled together in the cave, sharing a meager meal of scavenged vegetables and hardtack, the taste barely noticeable over the tension filling the air. Rebecca broke the silence, her voice soft but inviting.

"George, where are you from? How did you end up here in Vicksburg?"

George paused, setting down his small portion. A weary expression crossed his face, one born of a lifetime of hardship and resilience.

"I was born a slave, miss," his voice a murmur. "Been one all my life. Joseph Emory Davis, brother to Jefferson Davis, he brought me here from a plantation in Louisiana when I was just a boy."

Rebecca leaned in, her tone warm and respectful. "I am so sorry, George. Do you know where your family is?"

"No, ma'am," he replied, shaking his head slowly. "When Mr. Davis brought me to Hurricane Plantation, I was too small to remember much. Worked the fields mostly, tried to do right by folks around me. Then, one day, the Davises just left for Alabama—left us all there like we did not matter. My uncle, the man who raised me, he promised he would come back to fetch me, too, but he never did."

George's voice held a mix of sorrow and resilience as he continued. "When they left, I had no one to turn to. We tried to make the food last. For a little while, I even stayed in that big house they left behind. Then word came that the Feds were on their way to burn it down. I grabbed what little I could carry and ran."

He paused, eyes distant with memories. "When the Union soldiers came, and the house was just ashes and smoke, I fled here to Vicksburg, thinkin' maybe I'd find some sort of safety." His voice softened, filled with a hint of irony. "Well, here I am, with the city comin' down around my ears. Miss Mary's husband helped me get by, gave me work when he could. That is how I made it this far."

Rebecca listened, her heart heavy with the weight of his story. His tale of abandonment and survival stirred something deep within her, and the mention of Davis struck a familiar note. She kept her face composed as her mind raced. George's story of being left behind, of surviving on his own, was tragically familiar, yet his specific details held a strange resonance.

Later, when she was alone, Rebecca reached for a small notebook hidden in her skirt pocket. This was no ordinary notebook—it contained a list of names that John Scobell had shared with her, names of enslaved people he searched for, and, if possible, bring out of Mississippi. She flipped through the pages, her eyes skimming until she found a familiar name.

George.

Next to his name was a note about his last known location at Hurricane Plantation, with a brief mention of his potential as an informant. Rebecca traced her finger over the entry, feeling the gravity of the words settle over her. George was not just a forager trying to survive; he was a key piece in the mission. And, unknowingly, he was part of something larger than either of them.

As she closed the notebook, a new resolve grew within her. She would need to speak to George again, not merely as a friend sharing a meal in the dark, but as an ally, someone who deserved to know his significance in the fight for freedom. George had unknowingly contributed more than he realized, and he deserved to understand how much he meant to the cause.

She approached him the next evening, choosing her words. "George, there's something you should know." She kept her voice low. "You may think you are just surviving, but there is a reason you are still here, right here, at this moment. There is a reason we met. And it is because you are valuable. Your knowledge, your courage—it is all part of something much larger than either one of us."

George looked at her, a flicker of surprise mingling with a deep understanding in his eyes. In that quiet moment, surrounded by the distant rumble of war, Rebecca made a silent vow. She would help him see his own strength, his own importance, in a way that went beyond survival. Together, perhaps, they could create something beyond this nightmare, something that would matter.

*   *   *

That evening, as the cave fell quiet and the distant rumble of artillery fire faded into the night, Rebecca approached George. She chose her words with care, knowing that what she was about to say could change his life forever.

"George, have you ever dreamed about freedom?" she began, her voice gentle but purposeful. "About using what you know to help bring an end to this war?"

George looked at her, surprise flickering in his eyes, replaced by wariness. "What are you saying, miss?" he asked, suspicion mixed with a spark of curiosity.

Rebecca took a steadying breath, ready to invite him for a larger purpose. She could see that George, though weary, carried within him a hope buried deep beneath years of servitude—a hope she intended to reignite.

"George," she continued, her voice low, "do you have any family who might have made it north?"

George's hands stilled, and he held his breath. Finally, he spoke, his voice a whisper. "My uncle… the one I told you about. But I never knew if he was safe, or if he had really made it to a free state."

Rebecca leaned in, her gaze steady on his. "George, he made it. He is safe, and he's waiting for you. And there are people here who want to help you reach him. They are looking for you—they sent me to find you, to bring you to safety and freedom."

A light of astonished hope dawned in George's eyes, tempered by the weight of a lifetime of doubts. "You mean… there's really a way for me?" he asked, as though afraid to give shape to the dream he had held in secret for so long.

Rebecca nodded, her smile encouraging. "Yes, George. More than a way—a plan. And if you are willing, there is something you can do to help make it happen. You are not just a survivor; you are someone who could make a real difference."

George's gaze sharpened as her words sank in. "What do you mean?"

"You know these Confederate supply routes, where they're stockpiling resources," Rebecca said. "That knowledge could be a weapon in the right hands. If you can get word to the Union lines, it could change things, and it would show them the lengths you are willing to go for freedom."

A faint smile tugged at the corners of George's mouth, a mix of pride and disbelief. "You really think I could help the Federals?"

Rebecca placed a hand on his arm, her eyes earnest. "I know you can. And they will see it, too. When this siege is over, they will recognize what you've done, and you'll have earned not only your freedom but a future."

A slow, powerful resolve took hold of George's expression, and his shoulders, always heavy with unseen burdens, seemed to straighten with new purpose. "All right," he said, his voice steady and full of determination. "I will do whatever I can. Tell me what needs to be done."

"Just be ready," Rebecca replied, her own spirit lifted by his courage. "When the time comes, we will make our move. And I will be right there with you."

George nodded, the glimmer of hope in his eyes now a steady fire. "Thank you, Mrs. For the first time, freedom does not just feel like a dream. I will do my part. I will not let you down."

They shared a look of understanding, a silent promise of trust and purpose that bound them together in their shared fight. In that moment, George was not just a forager scraping by; he was a vital part of a larger mission, his spirit rekindled, his strength renewed by the hope of freedom that was no longer just a distant dream but an imminent, hard-won reality.

∗   ∗   ∗

The citizens of Vicksburg starved for news, cut off from the world beyond their besieged city. Information was scarce and unreliable, shared through whispers, rumors, and the occasional desperate letter smuggled in or out. Mary Loughborough often voiced her frustration and fear. "No one seems to know," she would say, her voice thin with anxiety and eyes almost wild, "whether the Federal army is advancing or if we will ever see relief. It is as if the world has forgotten us."

Rebecca felt those days stretching endlessly, pressing down on her with a kind of weight that made every breath heavy. She huddled in the cave, a thin blanket around her shoulders, listening to the same maddening silence that settled over Vicksburg each night, broken by the relentless shelling. In the darkness, Mary's voice would echo, full of hopelessness. "I shall never forget this terror," she murmured one night, her voice trembling. "I lie here, wondering if we'll see morning light, feeling like I'm already a ghost in this earth."

251

The ground trembled, and each explosion sent shockwaves through the cave, rattling every nerve. The terror was almost unbearable, the air thick with dread. Yet the spirit of Vicksburg's women and children refused to break. Defiance wove through their fear, and even spoke with pride that bordered on fierce rebellion.

"Let them think their shelling will wear us down," one woman declared, her voice rising above the rumble of artillery. "They think they will break us by battering women, children, and the sick. But rather than show them our suffering, I would sooner martyr myself. We Vicksburg women do not scare so easily!"

Rebecca marveled at the resilience she saw in these women. They faced unimaginable hardship, yet they clung to their pride and defiance with remarkable strength. Even as rumors of surrender began to circulate, the women held their heads high. One afternoon, a woman rushed back from the city center, an indignant laugh on her lips. "They are saying a handful of our own have dared to ask General Pemberton to surrender. Ha! Only three people signed it! Three!" She laughed, though it was a sound edged with desperation.

Yet others clung to a flickering hope that reinforcements would come, that Jefferson Davis or

General Johnston would arrive with troops to break the siege. Rumors spread like wildfire—Johnston's men in Tennessee would soon march south to liberate them, they said. "Any day now," someone whispered, though each day stretched into weeks, and no relief appeared on the horizon.

Rebecca watched as hope faltered and anger simmered, a dangerous mixture that made the city's spirit feel like a thread stretched too tight, about to snap. Through it all, the citizens of Vicksburg held onto the dignity of survival, their eyes fixed on the slim hope that they would one day break free from this nightmare, that they would endure long enough to see an end.

In those dark hours, huddled in the cave, Rebecca felt the weight of their desperation and courage pressing down on her, their hope and fear mingling with her own. The surrounding women, battered but unyielding, gave her strength, and as another night of shelling began, she tightened her hold on the blanket and whispered to herself a quiet promise: that she, too, would endure.

*　　*　　*

One afternoon, as Rebecca sat with Mary in a quiet corner of the city, a vendor's call rang out down the narrow, dusty street, a lifeline in a place where hope was as scarce as food. The man carried a small sack over his shoulder, his voice hoarse from exhaustion and dust.

"Pea meal and rice flour! Best you will find in Vicksburg!" he called, his voice cracking.

Rebecca and Mary exchanged a hopeful glance. Their rations were depleted, and though their coins were few, they couldn't ignore the slim chance to secure even a little more food. With their remaining coins in hand, the two women approached him.

The vendor looked them over with weary but sharp eyes. "What'll it be, ladies?"

Mary held out their few coins, her voice almost pleading. "Just a little of each… if you can spare it."

He shook his head, a sad smile flickering on his face. "At these prices, this will not buy more than a handful. Food's scarcer than gold around here."

Mary's shoulders slumped, and Rebecca felt a familiar helplessness settle over her—a feeling as constant now as the shelling. They looked down at their meager coins, realizing how far they had stretched them and how little they were worth now. With a sigh, Mary turned to leave, her disappointment clear.

As they started to walk away, the vendor's voice stopped Rebecca. She looked back, and he motioned her closer. Glancing around to ensure no one was watching, he slipped a small, sealed envelope into her hand.

"Get this to Pemberton," he murmured. "And don't let anyone else see it."

Rebecca's heart quickened as she slipped the envelope into her pocket, nodding in silent understanding. The vendor straightened and resumed his calls for pea meal and rice flour as if nothing had happened. Rebecca caught up to Mary, who had not noticed the exchange.

Back in the cave, as Mary settled into the corner, Rebecca found a quiet spot to examine the envelope. She broke the seal, unfolding the paper that bore the faint, musty scent of dust and ink. The letter, hastily scrawled, the handwriting uneven and urgent:

"General Pemberton, our rations have been cut down to one biscuit and a sliver of bacon per day, barely enough to keep a man alive, let alone fit for duty. If you can't feed us, you had better surrender us, horrible as the idea may be… This army is near mutiny unless it can be fed."

Signed simply, "Many Soldiers."

Rebecca felt a wave of mixed emotions as she absorbed the message. She recognized the words as Union propaganda, designed to weaken Pemberton's resolve, pushing him closer to surrender. And yet, the desperate appeal struck a chord within her. She had seen the suffering firsthand: gaunt, hollow-eyed soldiers and civilians alike, limping through the streets, faces drawn with hunger and fatigue. The harsh truth in the letter was undeniable.

She refolded the paper slowly, her fingers trembling with a mix of anger and empathy. If there was even a chance this letter could make Pemberton understand the reality his men and citizens faced, it was worth the risk to deliver it. This might be the way to end the suffering and bring peace to this place.

Determined, she tucked the letter back into her pocket and found George near the cave entrance, where he was standing watch.

"George," she whispered, holding out the letter, her gaze serious. "This needs to get to Pemberton. It is from his own men, urging him to surrender if he can't feed them. He must see it."

George took the letter, his expression shifting from surprise to understanding. "You think this'll change anything?" he asked, voice low.

Rebecca's voice softened, but her resolve remained steady. "Maybe. It is dangerous to carry, but if there's even a chance this could end the siege, it's worth it."

George nodded, slipping the letter into his vest. "I'll make sure he gets it," he promised.

Rebecca placed a hand on his arm, feeling the weight of the risk he was about to take. "Thank you, George. Be careful."

Without another word, he slipped into the shadows, blending with the night as he made his way through the war-torn streets. Rebecca stayed behind in the cave, her heart pounding, each second stretching into an eternity. She listened for any sounds of alarm, any distant shouts from the soldiers. But there was silence, interrupted by the occasional rumble of artillery from the hills.

Hours later, George returned, his face drawn but calm. He gave her a single nod. "It has been done. I left it right where he will find it."

Rebecca felt a wave of relief, tempered by the ever-present tension that had become her constant companion. She managed a small smile, and they shared a look of quiet understanding. They had taken a risk together, a dangerous act that might just shift the tide of the siege.

As the night wore on and the distant thunder of shelling resumed, Rebecca clung to a fragile hope. She knew the letter, crafted to manipulate Pemberton, a tactical play from the Union to push him toward surrender. Yet, as she listened to the shelling, it felt like more than propaganda. It felt like a necessary truth, a reflection of the suffering she saw around her every day.

If Pemberton could see it—if he could look beyond his pride and see the suffering of his men, women, and children—this siege could end.

In the cave's stillness, with George beside her, Rebecca allowed herself, just for a moment, to believe that peace might not be so far away.

Chapter Fourteen

On July 3rd, a new sight rose over the Confederate lines—a flag of truce flying against the smoke-streaked sky. The news swept through the Union ranks, stirring a cautious wave of relief. "Maybe this nightmare is ending," Wales murmured, sharing the thought with Thomas and John as they discussed the rumors of surrender. The idea brought a conflicted mix of emotions: relief that the suffering might end, sorrow for those who would not live to see it.

Yet through it all, Wales's kept circling back to Rebecca. Her courage, her dedication to the cause, and the invaluable information she had risked her life to gather had left a profound mark on him. But her absence gnawed at him, a hollow ache beneath the noise and chaos of war. Each blast, each story of suffering and survival, reminded him of what she— and all of them—endured in the fragile hope of peace.

As he looked out over the battered city, his resolve strengthened. He would find her when this was over, and he would do whatever it took to give her a life beyond the ruin of war. When the

Confederate flag came down, he would be there, ready to rebuild something that went beyond survival—a life free from hunger, fear, and suffering.

On July 4th, 1863, Wales, Samuel Peppers, and John Scobell stood among the Union ranks, watching the scene with a tense silence. There were no festivities, no cheers—only the solemn gathering of soldiers whose faces etched with fatigue. From their vantage, they saw Confederate General John C. Pemberton step forward to meet General Ulysses S. Grant. The two men, once fierce opponents, exchanged words that carried the weight of countless lives lost and the bitter divide of the war.

Wales watched, half-listening to the murmurs around him, his eyes searching the procession of Confederate soldiers emerging from Vicksburg. Rebecca's face did not appear among them. He swallowed hard, feeling his pulse throb with a mixture of dread and steely determination. She must be here somewhere. He was clinging to the hope that she'd survived.

John Scobell leaned in close, his gaze sharp and steady. "Been a long time coming, hasn't it, Wales?"

Wales nodded, still scanning the stream of soldiers filing past, surrendering their weapons in grim silence. Samuel Peppers, standing at his other side, let out a low whistle. "Hard to believe it is over. But I haven't seen Corporal Humphrey yet, either. Odd, don't you think?"

Wales's frown deepened as he realized Humphery was missing. The corporal had been close to their unit, sharing in the burdens of command and the grind of the siege. His absence now, at this pivotal moment, stirred Wales's unease. "Yes…strange." He continued scanning the crowd as the defeated Confederate soldiers moved past like a slow river.

As Pemberton signed the official surrender, shaking hands with Grant, a ripple of cheers swept through the Union lines. For most, it was a moment of triumph, an end to hardship. But for Wales, it felt like the beginning of another kind of battle. With Vicksburg open to them at last, he had one mission on his mind: to find Rebecca.

Stepping over piles of rubble and past shattered homes, he pushed forward, his heart racing as he replayed every memory of their last encounter. It had been weeks since he had watched her disappear across the lines, her form slipping into the hills under a haze of dust and cannon smoke. Since then, he had had no word, and each passing day had darkened his hope, leaving him with the gnawing fear that she could be lost forever, buried beneath the rubble of Vicksburg.

Samuel and John kept pace with him, their eyes sharp and their steps unwavering. Sensing his friend's turmoil, Samuel clapped him on the back. "We'll find Albert, Wales," he said, using Rebecca's alias. "Vicksburg's ours now, and if anyone can survive what it's been through, it's Albert."

Wales managed a nod, his eyes flashing with grim determination. He would search every war-torn street, investigate every battered shelter, question every weary face if he had to. Vicksburg was theirs now, and he intended to leave no stone unturned until he found her.

As they moved through the devastated city, Wales could not shake the feeling of foreboding that hung over him. It was a tension that lay beyond the crumbling walls and hollow-eyed survivors, something he could not define. The people of Vicksburg staggered around him, faces etched with hunger and loss, struggling to comprehend the end of the siege and the beginning of a new hardship.

But Wales pushed all of it aside. He could not rest, could not let go, until he found her. His heart pounded as he continued down the ruined streets, consumed by Rebecca. Each step forward was one step closer, and he clung to the hope that, somewhere in the shadows of this battered city, she was waiting, as determined to survive as he was to find her.

*   *   *

When they lied to Samuel telling him they sent Albert to pick up supplies sent down the Mississippi River north of Vicksburg a few weeks ago, they included that they had not intended for "Albert" to go into the besieged city. His task had been simple: retrieve supplies from a designated drop point just outside Vicksburg, far enough, they had thought, to avoid the worst of the Confederate artillery.

But things had not gone as planned. Word reached the camp that the shelling had intensified along the outskirts, scattering civilians and anyone unfortunate enough to be nearby. Samuel had put two and two together and since they heard nothing from Albert, worry crept into every corner of Samuel's mind.

Samuel, walking beside him as they searched for Albert in Vicksburg, muttered, his frustration plain.

"I just do not get it, Wales. Why would they send Albert to get supplies in such a dangerous spot? It was not worth risking him over a few barrels of flour or sacks of rice. We need him too much." Samuel shook his head, his brows knitting together. "And now he has gone missing? It is plain stupid."

Wales knew Samuel's frustration was not without reason. Samuel couldn't understand why "Albert" had been sent so close to enemy territory for what seemed like a simple supply pickup, and Wales wished he could tell him about the real purpose behind Rebecca's errand. But Samuel did not know the truth about 264blert, and he couldn't know that the trip had been about more than supplies.

"We didn't expect the shelling to hit so close to the drop," Wales said, keeping his voice steady through the lie, though he shared every bit of Samuel's frustration. "They will send word if he has made it to any of the outer camps. He is resourceful—he'll find his way back."

Samuel huffed, unconvinced. "He better because it is not just his cooking we would miss. It is… him. We are lucky to have him, and I do not understand risking him like that."

Wales did not respond, the weight of guilt tightening in his chest. He knew Samuel would not understand the urgency of Rebecca's mission, could not fathom that her work was essential to the Union's progress. Yet none of that eased the strain of knowing she was out there, caught in siege, with no word of her whereabouts or safety.

"Keep up," Samuel muttered, but Wales was already ahead, pushing through the ruined streets with single-minded focus. He did not care about the looks he received from the weary Confederate soldiers or the disdainful glares from the remaining civilians—especially the Confederate women who stood defiantly with narrowed eyes and stony faces. To them, he was an intruder, the face of victory they refused to acknowledge. But none of that mattered to him now. All that mattered was finding her.

"Wales, I am going to check near the river," said Samuel and darted off before he could reply.

Wales barely registered his words, already striding toward the outskirts of town, where he had heard civilians might take shelter. The caves. If she were anywhere, it could be there, hiding or, worse, trapped, or…

He shook off the idea, his boots kicking up dust as he hurried past a group of ragged Confederate soldiers, heads low. His mind raced, replaying every memory of their last conversation. The look in her eyes when she had left camp. She had been so determined, so fearless, but that didn't stop him from worrying. He should have insisted on going with her. He should have—

"Wales."

The voice was faint but clear, cutting through the noise like a knife. He stopped, turning toward the sound. His heart leapt in his chest as his eyes locked on a familiar figure moving toward him, her steps slow but steady. His breath caught.

It was Rebecca.

She stood near the makeshift hospital, partially hidden between two battered buildings. Her dress stained and torn, her hair loose and tangled, but it was unmistakably her. Her right arm bandaged, her face etched with exhaustion and strain, but she was alive.

Wales looked around to ensure they were alone, then sprinted toward her, his emotions breaking free. When he reached her, he pulled her deeper into the alley and into his arms, holding her, afraid she might vanish again.

"You're alive," he whispered, his voice raw with relief.

Rebecca, though weak, managed a faint smile. "Barely," she said, her voice rough but steady. "But I'm here."

Wales pulled back just enough to look at her, his hands gripping her shoulders as if to confirm she was real. "I thought... I thought I had lost you."

Her eyes softened, and she raised her good hand to touch his face. "I am here, Wales. I made it. It was…horrible." Her voice broke, and she leaned into him, burying her face in his chest as her shoulders trembled. Wales held her, his own eyes damp as he stroked her hair, feeling the full weight of his worry dissolve in her presence.

"I've got you," he whispered, the words a quiet promise. For the first time in weeks, he felt as though he could breathe again.

Just then, a familiar voice broke the moment. "Found her, did you?"

Wales turned to see Corporal Thomas Humphery emerging from the shadows nearby, his face lined with exhaustion but softened by a small, approving smile. His voice was low, but it held a note of satisfaction. "She is a sight, isn't she? I spotted her near the hospital, barely recognizable under all that dust and grime, but I knew she would make her way there."

Wales looked up, gratitude in his eyes. "Thank you, Thomas. I owe you."

Thomas nodded; his gaze warm. "It's good to see her alive." He cast a knowing look at Rebecca. "She's been through hell, but she's here now."

At that moment, another figure appeared behind Thomas—a familiar woman with a frazzled look and a young Black man beside her. Mary Webster Loughborough rushed forward; her voice laced with relief. "Alice!" she exclaimed, her arms reaching out before she paused, noticing how Wales held her friend.

Rebecca managed a weary smile. "Mary."

Mary hesitated, her eyes flickering with a mix of realization and gratitude. "You're not who you said you were, are you, Alice?" Her tone was soft, almost amused. She glanced between Rebecca and Wales, as if putting the pieces together. "But no matter. I do not know what I would've done without you."

Rebecca's eyes softened. "Mary, I—"

Mary waved a hand, dismissing the unspoken apology. "Honestly, Alice—whoever you are, I don't care. I never would have made it through without you."

Mary's eyes shifted to Wales, a warm but wary look on her face. "Captain, thank you for keeping her safe. She has been a rock for me through all of this."

Then, she nodded toward George, who stood by her side, clutching his hat. "And thank you for helping George as well."

Wales glanced at the young man, nodding. Thomas cleared his throat and stepped forward, looking at George. "You will be safe with us, George. And I have a friend nearby—John Scobell. He will be thrilled to see you and help you get back north, if that's what you want."

George's eyes lit up with a glimmer of hope. "Mr. Scobell? Here?"

Thomas nodded. "Not far. We will get you to him."

Mary's face softened as she gave George's hand a reassuring squeeze. "You have been a rock for me, too, George. I am forever grateful."

Rebecca took Mary's hands in hers, her eyes shining with gratitude. "Mary, you were my friend through the darkest of times. Thank you for everything."

Mary pulled Rebecca into a brief, fierce embrace, her voice thick with emotion. "Take care, my Alice. You have saved me in more ways than you know."

Thomas stepped in, ready to escort Mary and George. "Come along, Mrs. Loughborough. We will make sure you are reunited with your husband." He turned to Rebecca, his tone gentle. "Rest up, Private. You are among friends now."

With one last look of gratitude, Mary and George disappeared into the ruins of Vicksburg with Thomas as their guide. When they were gone, Wales and Rebecca were left in the quiet aftermath of their reunion, surrounded by the muffled noise of a city in surrender.

As the first light of dawn spilled over the shattered city, casting long shadows across the rubble-strewn streets, Wales held Rebecca close, feeling the relief of finding her alive mingling with a new determination. In his heart, he had made a decision: this was her last mission. Whatever it took, he would send her back to safety, back to a life where danger wasn't lurking around every corner.

"Rebecca," he began, his voice carrying a gentle but firm resolve. "When we leave this place, you are going home. I cannot... I won't see you in harm's way like this again. It is time to leave this war behind."

Rebecca pulled back, just enough to look him in the eyes. There was surprise in her expression, followed by something defiant, even amusing. "Go home?" she echoed, a faint smile touching her lips. "Wales, you know me better than that by now."

He felt his jaw tighten, the flicker of a frustrated smile crossing his face. "I do know you. And that is why I am saying this. You have done more than anyone could have asked of you. You have risked your life over and over. It is time for a fresh start, far from here."

Her smile faded, replaced by a spark of stubborn resolve. "And do what, Wales? Sit in some parlor and pretend I have not seen what I have seen? Felt what I have felt?" She shook her head. "You may think this is where it ends for me, but it is not. I belong here—there is a thrill in the work, a purpose I cannot ignore. I am not done yet."

Wales clenched his fists, struggling to keep his frustration in check. "And what about the risk? The possibility that one day, you will not come back. You have seen the cost of all this, Rebecca. I have seen it. I cannot bear losing you— not like this."

She reached up, touching his face, her gaze steady. "I know the risks, Wales. And I accept them. I would not ask you to change it for me, so do not ask me to turn away from this now. This… this is my life as much as yours."

He shook his head, torn between his desire to keep her safe and the reality that she was as stubborn as he was. "I do not want to watch you disappear into the shadows again. I want more for you."

Rebecca's eyes softened, but her resolve was unwavering. "Do not send me away. I am not a delicate thing to be tucked out of sight."

Wales sighed, feeling the weight of her conviction. This was not a battle he could win, not now. And, as much as it frustrated him, he could not deny the admiration he felt for her spirit, for the very resolve that had drawn him to her in the first place. The struggle between them would remain, he knew, but for now, he could only nod, his resistance softening into reluctant acceptance.

"Fine," he murmured, his voice low. "But promise me this: when the time comes to go, you will leave this life behind."

She smiled, her hand tightening in his. "When that day comes, Wales, I'll be right beside you."

For now, they were bound by both adventure and conflict, the shared thrill and danger that neither could quite walk away from. As they left the ruins of Vicksburg behind, he realized their journey was far from over—and, for better or worse, they would face it together.

ABOUT THE AUTHOR

Paula Lenor Webb is an accomplished author, librarian, and community advocate known for her dedication to storytelling and education. A native of Mobile, Alabama, Paula has written extensively about Southern history, blending meticulous research with compelling narratives. Her work often explores untold stories, shining a light on the diverse voices that shaped the region's past.

Paula's creativity, warmth, and commitment to preserving history make her a valued member of the Mobile community. Whether organizing events, mentoring students, or crafting her next book, Paula's work reflects her love for the stories that connect us all.

www.ingramcontent.com/pod-product-compliance
Lightning Source LLC
Chambersburg PA
CBHW020137310726
48970CB00006B/1907